A BAD INVESTMENT

a novel by

Ed Bonner

bonner.edwin@gmail.com

ISBN: 9798884707481
Imprint: Independently published

"Money may be the husk of many things, but not the kernel.

It brings you food, but not appetite; medicine, but not health; acquaintances, but not friends; servants, but not faithfulness;

days of joy, but not peace or happiness."

—Henrik Ibsen

"If money go before, all ways do lie open."

The Merry Wives of Windsor

—William Shakespeare

"Money does not change people, it unmasks them."

—Henry Ford

"No one in this world can you trust. Not men, not women, not beasts.
Crush your enemies, see them driven before you."

—Conan the Barbarian (1982)

"From childhood's hour I have not been
As others were; I have not seen
As others saw; I could not bring
My passions from a common spring.
From the same source I have not taken
My sorrow; I could not awaken
My heart to joy at the same tone;
And all I loved, I loved alone."

— Alone — Edgar Allan Poe

A Bad Investment

23rd March 2022

Dearest Carol & Stewart

I hope you enjoy this work

Much love

Ed

Table of Contents

Chapter 1 An Unattractive Boy 1

Chapter 2 The Chess Wars 7

Chapter 3 *Krav Maga* 13

Chapter 4 The Student Years 17

Chapter 5 The Property Mogul 21

Chapter 6 *Illegitimi Non Carborundum* 29

Chapter 7 The Scheissters 37

Chapter 8 Opportunities 47

Chapter 9 Daniel Odenfemji 51

Chapter 10 Spanish Clouds 59

Chapter 11 Sanguivorous? 65

Chapter 12 La Dolce Vita 69

Chapter 13 Bubbles: The Subprime Debacle 75

Chapter 14 Happiness? 79

Chapter 15 Chloe Jenkins 83

Chapter 16 The King's Ransom 93

Chapter 17 Karl Janssens 95

Chapter 18 Carmen 103

Chapter 19 The French Deal 113

Chapter 20 The Big Apple 117

Chapter 21 Music to Karl's Ears 125

Chapter 22 A Doctor and A Lawyer... 129

Chapter 23 A Big Deal 137

Chapter 24 Invitation For A Pizza 141

Chapter 25 Milano 145

Chapter 26 Chloe Pulls the Plug 155

Chapter 27 Cybercrime 159

Chapter 28 Santa Fe 165

Chapter 29 A Breakthrough 169

Chapter 30 The Prostate Gland 173

Chapter 31 The Game Unfolds 181

Chapter 32 A Very Nasty Letter 185

Chapter 33 Endgame 197

Chapter 34 The Endgame Ends 203

Chapter 35 Aftermath 215

Chapter 36 Postscript 221

Acknowledgements 229

About the Author 231

Chapter 1
An Unattractive Boy

Jeremy Lawson was extremely rich and had been for a very long time. He was also unattractive and had been for even longer. Always conscious of his less than handsome appearance and well before he became very wealthy, Jeremy decided early in his life that he would not fight his unattractiveness.

Early in his life? Is age six early enough? That was how old he was when he attempted to hold the hand of a little girl in his class. Her name was Shelley. Shelley had pulled her hand away with a grimace and hissed, "I don't *want* to hold your hand. I don't like you."

"Why don't you like me?"

"My mummy says you look like a bulldog - and you do!" said the affronted little girl.

Truth to tell, that is how he had always appeared: short and squat; somewhat stout although not fat; jowly, even at an early age; large lugubrious lips. On the credit side he did have masses of brown wavy hair, but this did not seem to weigh sufficiently in his favour.

Jeremy did not burst into tears as a more emotional child might have done. He might not have been emotional, but he was undoubtedly sensitive, and sensitive children hurt easily. He simply withdrew his hand and walked away from little Shelley. Until that moment, it had never entered Jeremy's mind that his appearance might be a determinant in whether another child might wish to befriend him. Why was what he looked like important to this little girl? Then, even in his young mind, he worked out that the reason he had wanted to hold *her* hand in the first place was that he thought she was pretty. She had not wanted to hold *his* because he looked like a bulldog. If he looked like a spaniel, would she have wanted to befriend him? Quite likely.

This little six-year-old boy had just learned a couple of important life lessons: first, that one's appearance *was* important; second, that he had just engaged in a battle, and he had lost. He had lost because it was a battle where the advantage was not on his side and probably never would be. Therefore, better not to have engaged.

Shelley's nasty (if true) words were to have a bigger influence on his life than he ever could have envisaged. Following that episode of unrequited warmth to a member of the opposite sex, Jeremy made a conscious decision that he would never again place himself in a situation where such an event might occur again. One might say that a sample of one was insufficient evidence on which to base a philosophy of life, but one was one too many for the sensitive little six-year-old. From that day, Jeremy shunned any thought of attempting to create a relationship with a girl or later a woman.

Jeremy returned home and related what had happened to his mother. "Mum, why did she say such nasty things? I don't think it's fair, Mummy, it's just *not fair*."

Grace was an artist who rarely took much time to shower attention on anything other than her canvasses. His parents always had music going (often on dusty vinyl) as their only companion in their lonesome studios. On this occasion however, aware of his hurt, she turned off the record player, enveloped her only child and smothered the small boy with kisses.

"Life is not always fair, darling, but don't worry. One day, when you are the handsomest, richest man in the world, that silly nasty Shelley will be so, so sorry she wasn't nice to you."

Was he any happier getting along with boys? In a word, no. He had no greater predilection for members of the same sex than he had for girls, but perhaps for better reason. Boys who are good at sport tend to be happier, more popular, and more confident than those who are not, and Jeremy was not good at sport. Being slightly portly was not generally conducive to being quick nor to having the ability to control a ball on the move. He tried playing goalkeeper, but his lack of height counted against him, and in any case, he had an unfortunate tendency to drop the ball at crucial moments. As a consequence, whenever teams were being picked for a kickaround in the playground during break or after school, more often than not Jeremy found himself the last to be selected.

After one occasion when he allowed the football to go into goal through his splayed legs, the other boys would not allow him to participate at all. He was shunned. Being a child who was slighted easily, he found this galling.

The final straw was when the football master said to him, "Lawson, you couldn't kick the skin off a rice pudding! For gawd's sake, laddie, put a bit of wellie into your kicking!" He saw no point in trying to please the football master by trying harder to kick harder. As for the boys, they didn't want to play with him? Pah! He didn't need boys. He certainly didn't need football or cricket or whatever other silly games boys played, so sport and boys were added to his proscribed list alongside girls.

It was a similar story with his cousins, few though they were. He was far brighter than they and tended to outsmart them in any game where intellect rather than strength was required. He especially liked Monopoly. To some extent Monopoly is a game of chance: the dice determine where you land and whether you 'advance to -' or 'go back to -', but even at a young age Jeremy showed acumen in choosing which properties to buy, whether to build, and when to sell. He had the mind to calculate that some properties gave a better return on investment than others - not bad for an eight-year-old! He enjoyed the notion that it was within his power to drive his opponents into bankruptcy, something he did more often than not. They would try to leave the table, then be told by a parent to sit and watch and learn from Jeremy's tactics. Jeremy liked that.

Whenever a game of Monopoly or Scrabble or any other contest requiring intellectual prowess was being considered when families got together at Christmas or on birthdays, he would inevitably be left out because those cousins hated losing almost as much as they disliked him.

So, when girls don't like you, boys don't want you to play with them, and family can't manage your cleverness, you have to adapt. That is the Darwinian way. To protect himself, Jeremy developed the thickest of skins. He became nothing if not resilient. If other boys and girls did not wish to have him play with them, he would learn to get on with things himself – an early and valuable lesson in managing the vicissitudes of life.

As events turned out, half of his mother's prognostication would come true, because Jeremy did become extremely rich. And, as he grew wealthier, his unattractive features seemed to diminish until they became a non-factor in his life.

Chapter 2
The Chess Wars

As Jeremy progressed through school not being adept at outdoor games, he learned to be excellent at those indoor. He joined the school chess club, quickly picking up the rudiments and then the refinements of the complex game. What appealed to him was the realisation that chess was more than a game - it was a battle. Not a battle determined by one's appearance or fleetness of foot or ability to strike a ball; rather by mental agility, concentration and adaptation, and these were assets he possessed in abundance. Chess was a contest of strategy, a battle of wits. In battles of the mind, he could be king; and if he was king, what better army to have at your disposal than chess pieces? Chess after all was nothing more or less than an intense fight to the death between the armies of kingdoms. Once a king is trapped, the game is over. To protect his king (himself) and conquer his enemy, he had to be astute, sharp and guileful. There were times when one had to sacrifice a soldier or even an officer in order to improve one's position, but this had to be done mercilessly and with cunning. As his metaphorical army's leader, he had to plan every move well in advance, and when the plan was executed, there was no margin for error. Jeremy had the ability to ensure that his kingdom would prevail.

This was fertile territory for the young man. He developed a quiet determination to succeed whatever the opposition and had never yet met anyone who could outsmart him, certainly not on the chessboard. Soon he had the beating of opponents several years older than he, and the ruthless efficiency with which he dispatched them did not endear him to the other members of the chess club. It was no surprise when they turned down every opportunity to have a game with him, yet perversely were happy to have him on their team to play other schools.

The upshot of this was that Jeremy was forced to discover that chess was a game for two that could be also played by one. He would spend hours in his room playing both black and white. This taught him not only how to plan to attack opponents but also how to defend by anticipating their likely moves. He learned to think strategically many moves ahead, to assess risk, especially later when pitting his wits against computerised opposition. He was not a computer but taught himself to think like one - quickly and in binary terms. 'Move A', sound; 'move B', complicated, therefore higher risk of error – calculate the consequences of that risk. The life lessons he learned from chess would serve him well many years later in legal matters and business deals.

His parents had learned not to push him to be more gregarious and outgoing. They accepted he could be happy on his own, and in this he was much like them. They were moderately successful artists who spent most days closeted in their own studios. Mealtimes tended to be reflective rather than chatty, the topics of discussion usually related to current events or what they were reading, and especially to the sales progress of their works. To their credit, Jeremy was never left out of a conversation, and began to think like an adult long before he became one.

Although they were physically warm neither to each other nor to him, Jeremy did not feel unloved, and certainly felt respected, which redressed the balance somewhat and gave him a useful degree of self-confidence. What Jeremy Lawson had also in his favour was a very sharp little brain that grew into a very astute big brain as he grew older.

Being alone so much, even as a child he read a great deal - not just children's or teenagers' books, but adult stories, novels and magazines. He loved the stories of Greek heroes: Homer's Odyssey and the tale of Odysseus and Penelope; Tennyson's Ulysses. Difficult reading for a young boy? Jeremy devoured them. He would be inspired to write his own tales of bullies brought low - epics of the loner triumphant. He kept those stories to himself, allowing not even his parents to read them. What became of those is unknown. None was ever published – he had no desire to share the creations of his mind with anyone else.

He loved books that had a moral spine, especially when the protagonist was able to succeed against overwhelming odds.

As he reached his teens, he read everything that Dickens, Twain, Conan Doyle and Steinbeck had to offer, and loved none more than East of Eden. *'All great and precious things are lonely'* was the phrase that lingered long in his mind. Steinbeck would always be the writer Jeremy would have wished to have write his biography.

"Jeremy, it's rude to read at the table."

"Sorry Dad, but I have to know what's going to happen."

His father glanced at the library book's title: *The Catcher in the Rye.* It didn't mean much to him, but it did to his thirteen-year-old son. Salinger's book had a profound influence on Jeremy's developing character, and he identified strongly with its teenage protagonist Holden Caulfield. Although Holden was intelligent and sensitive, he narrated the story in a cynical and jaded voice. He found the hypocrisy and ugliness of the world around him almost intolerable, and through his cynicism tried to protect himself from the pain and disappointment of the adult world. Holden did not lose his virginity during the course of *The Catcher in the Rye*. Jeremy could easily identify with this but with a singular difference: though Holden made some half-hearted attempts to do so, Jeremy had no intention of following suit. Like Holden, Jeremy found himself increasingly intolerant of the insincerity of many in his peer group, especially those boasting of conquests. There are very few people who are less forgiving than a teenager sniffing out inauthenticity, and Jeremy, like Caulfield, could smell it all around him.

Then he located *The Fountainhead* on his parents' bookshelf. It looked daunting. "Do you think I'll enjoy this, Dad?"

"I'm not sure. Ayn Rand's heavy on promoting individuality and full-on capitalism - a bit like you really, but if you can get through it, I'm sure you'll find it absorbing."

The notion Ayn Rand's proponent Howard Roark embodied was that individualism was a more powerful force than collectivism. Not necessarily a trait to be desired or emulated, but the championing of individuality resonated powerfully within Jeremy's developing mind. One paragraph in particular became a tenet of his burgeoning philosophy of life: *"Man cannot survive but through his mind. He comes on earth unarmed. His brain is his only weapon .... everything we are and we have comes from a single attribute of man - the function of his reasoning mind."*

Jeremy copied that paragraph, had it printed and framed and placed above his desk.

Having words as his best and only friend, he learned to use them forcefully. He excelled in debating at school where he had the power to demolish lesser beings with just the right insight, quotation or epigram. There was no need for him to be nasty when he was able instead to be smart. Few ever left a discussion or argument with Jeremy not having had their fundamental beliefs shaken and feeling a little less clever than they had previously believed. Several teachers remarked to his parents that he already showed the hallmarks of an embryonic legal mind and foresaw a career in the law.

Chapter 3

Krav Maga

In stark contrast to the sentiment expressed by Howard Roark, Jeremy realised that at some point he would have to deal with physical bullying. One rather dim-witted boy had made a crass remark to him in class, to which Jeremy responded, "When you've no idea what you're speak"ing about, it's better to keep your mouth shut." The oaf, not entirely unreasonably, threatened to punch his lights out.

Being emotionally bullied was so much part of his life that he accepted it as normal - he had the wit to deal with that - but he abhorred being pushed around and not having the tools to retaliate. So, always trying to keep at least one step ahead he enrolled for training in *Krav Maga,* contact combat simultaneously using defensive and offensive manoeuvres. This system of self-defence had been developed for the Israeli Defence Force, and encompassed techniques of boxing and wrestling as well as karate, ju-jitsu and judo.

He hoped never to have to use these methods, but should the need ever arise, they would be there for him. He foresaw this happening sooner rather than later because he knew unpopularity when it stared him in the face – he'd certainly had enough practice!

A few of the boys in his class began to become even more aggressive towards him than he accepted as normal. They resented what they perceived as his overly superior attitude. One afternoon, three of the bully pack cornered him as he headed towards an imminent chess match. One began to jostle him, and it did not take long before the other two joined in. As the pack leader tried to swing a punch, Jeremy realised that all that stood between him and a sound beating was his Krav Maga training.

He parried the intended blow and at the same time forcefully jabbed his fingers into his tormentor's eyes. He then kneed the lout in his crotch and followed this with a chop to the soft hollow spot beneath the larynx. His assailant staggered before falling to the ground, coughing and retching. Sorted. The entire battle had lasted less than thirty seconds. Would his gawking buddies then pile in as any self-respecting bullies should have done? Not a chance. They picked up their comrade and dispersed as quickly as they had arrived, never to bother him again. Checkmate.

Jeremy began to invent little cheat-proof games that he could play against himself. Even before attending university, he patented one of these games that he called *'Jurisdiction!'* It became enormously successful when it was purchased by a major company for a not inconsiderable sum in a deal that included royalties. Jeremy negotiated the deal entirely on his own. The well-marketed game was to find its way into many homes at Christmas time. Had he never done another deal in his life or worked another day, he could have lived modestly on the proceeds of those royalties, but that was not Jeremy.

The director of the company was so impressed that he offered Jeremy a position so worthwhile that another person might have grabbed it voraciously. Jeremy, to the bemused concern of his parents, declined the offer because he preferred to plough his own furrow - he was not reliant on others, nor did he wish to be. He wanted to be in control of his own life and was not about to change that state. Howard Roark incarnate.

Chapter 4
The Student Years

The man who moves a mountain begins by carrying away small stones." —Confucius.

Jeremy decided to study at London University for the degree in law to which he seemed predestined and was so eminently suited. Or had initially thought he was. When the penny dropped that the legal world dealt with solving the problems of others, he realised that it was not a role he wished to play. He simply did not like those others sufficiently to want to sort out *their* issues. Not that he was misanthropic, or not more than he found absolutely necessary, but service to others ranked very low on his list of values.

Individualism. Entrepreneurship. Those were far more suited to his temperament. After attaining his bachelor's degree in jurisprudence, a useful foundation, he decided to read for a master's degree in finance and commerce at the London Business School in its magnificent location inside Regent's Park. He enjoyed and appreciated those lectures and seminars that related to pecuniary matters and market forces far more than those concerning behavioural science and cementing one's place in an organisational setting. He earned the grudging respect of his colleagues but not their love. It is not easy to be liked when you are the one who is gifted with a unique ability to boil down complex ideas into simple terms and regularly outsmart your peers.

As far as Jeremy was concerned, the company of his classmates was to be tolerated rather than enjoyed. He found no reason to join his group for essential extra-curricular activities such as meeting at a pub after lectures. He was often taciturn to the point of silence. One colleague actually asked him, not vindictively, whether he had ever considered life as a Trappist monk. No one actively disliked him, they just saw him as a person apart, and all were content to leave it that way.

It was at the business school that he acquired another great asset: an appreciation of the power of wealth, if not yet the acquisition of it. He remembered his mother's words those years ago: *one day, when you are the handsomest, richest man in the world....* He'd never be handsome, but he could aspire to extreme wealth, and he realised that was what he wanted more than anything. Even more than becoming the chess champion that was entirely within his power. He had gained understanding of a fundamental dogma of life: being a lawyer could win battles, but money won wars. He would become a warrior to be feared.

As a student, he discovered another game that suited his skills and temperament: bridge. Unlike chess, bridge was a social game, and involving himself in it had the effect of bringing Jeremy out of his inner-bound self, if only to a limited extent. It was as competitive as chess but in addition required great communication skills – never his forte, but one that of necessity he had to develop. He liked that bridge had two aspects: first, an auction where opposing pairs engaged in bidding for contracts. The bidding process required learning the conventions by which a great amount of information could be passed in just two or three words not only to one's partner but also to one's opponents.

The second phase involved playing the cards in a sequence based on the information obtained in the bidding process that would either win the contract or cause it to crash. It required prodigious memory and concentration in remembering which cards had already been played, and also the nous to make correct assumptions in whose hands the cards yet to be played would be likely to be located. Based on the bidding process, he did not find it taxing to work out who was holding what cards in which suit. Before he played his first card, he had already calculated the sequence in which the twelve cards that would follow should be played.

Participating at every opportunity, he became as adept at bridge as he was at chess. Bridge required attacking and defensive skills that, as with chess, would serve him well when, years later, he involved himself in business.

Jeremy could not possibly have anticipated the hand that karma was about to deal for him.

Chapter 5
The Property Mogul

"I would give a thousand furlongs of sea for an acre of barren ground"—William Shakespeare

"A simple rule dictates my buying: be fearful when others are greedy, be greedy when others are fearful." —Warren Buffett

Very soon after he completed his studies at the age of twenty-two, he lost both parents - his mother taken by unsuspected ovarian cancer, his father crushed by a truck while cycling in the city two months later. Jeremy had suddenly been orphaned and was completely alone. That he was saddened was beyond question, but not as emotionally damaged as another might have been. His thick carapace protected him and, as in the past, he would survive and grow stronger, reliant on no-one but himself.

It was that self that engaged with the trucker's insurance company and, following an extended court battle fought without legal assistance on his part, won a substantial pay-out. The lone bee was becoming a stinging hornet.

Jeremy had cause to be very grateful to his parents. They were not wealthy, but they had left him, their only child, a repository of unsold art. Three years before his dad's untimely death, one of his father's paintings had been selected for the Royal Academy Summer Exhibition, and his artwork had begun to escalate in value. The following year, his mother was accorded an exhibition at a private gallery with similar consequence. Their reputation and marketability soared. They had been shrewd enough to sell discriminately and not flood the market with their works. This lesson did not go unnoticed by their perceptive son.

They bequeathed unto him the house in Queen's Park where every available square foot of space was adorned with artwork escalating in value. When they originally bought that semi-detached house before Jeremy was born, it had been an inexpensive purchase in a nondescript street, not quite run-down but heading that way. Queen's Park, despite its grandiose moniker, was then a lowly-rated suburb within easy distance of Notting Hill Gate which, at the time, was definitely run-down and seedy. Notting Hill in the fifties was inhabited largely by exploited immigrants of the Windrush Generation: decent, hard-working people of West Indian origin who had arrived in hope and become the victims of what came to be known as Rachmanism, rent exploitation, not to mention extreme racism.

The fifties first ambled then galloped its way into the eighties. Because of its proximity to the West End, the attractive but overcrowded large houses in Notting Hill Gate had been identified as being better suited to wealthier denizens; the suburb was becoming increasingly gentrified, the properties within it more expensive. When Notting Hill prices became too rarefied for those of a more artistic or literary bent, Queen's Park proved a desirable next-best option, and the value of the Lawson house soared.

Property values had been rising steadily, so Jeremy made the decision to ride the bandwagon that was property investment. It is a truism that if you can see a bandwagon, you've probably missed it, but these were early days, and he foresaw lots of good mileage still available to be travelled.

If one is going to be a serious property dealer it seemed a good idea to purchase a property company, and Jeremy decided to follow this route. He named his trading company 'Aida', chosen after seeing a fine performance of the Verdi opera featuring Placido Domingo and Leontine Price, conducted by Herbert Von Karajan. That opera was the beginning of a long-lasting and consuming passion in serious music, and he hoped that honouring her name would be propitious. If he were superstitious, he would have considered that things did not end well for the operatic soprano, but Jeremy was not one to trust to luck, and his company was to fare a great deal better than the eponymous heroine.

With Aida Property Holdings as the vehicle, Jeremy began driving small investments, then speeding up the stakes when careful statistical analysis allowed him to feel comfortable. Academic finance is devoted to finding investment strategies that are mathematically optimal. Jeremy was not an academic - however, he thought like a human computer. He had a brain that could calculate the trade-off between risk and return accurately, quickly and reliably. Given the up-and-down nature of the markets and the economy, he did not allow himself to get into debt that could spiral out of control. He created more capital than he invested in a small but growing portfolio of assets.

For many, the eighties was a lucrative decade, especially in the USA. American investment banks began to move into areas of trade previously controlled by building societies and were more cavalier than the mortgagors in giving loans. Bankers like Lehman Bros and Bear Stearns had become the new Masters of the Universe. Jeremy did consider investing in American property but decided against it – it was a time when many British fashion retail companies had got badly burned fingers in the USA and he had no desire to add to the statistics in markets where he lacked experience.

This was a time to be buying at home, and with the assistance of several eager UK bankers Jeremy used his inheritance to do just that. Houses were relatively inexpensive - to give you an idea of values back then, the average house cost around four times average earnings; today, houses cost around nine times earnings.

The UK housing market enjoyed a period of sustained growth that was tied to the strong performance of the economy as a whole. This boom resulted from a combination of factors, in particular high productivity, low unemployment, and high inflation.

By 1988, the market was at its peak, but there were clear signs that the boom was coming to an end. After her initial successes, Margaret Thatcher's gloss was beginning to look tarnished due to her attempt to introduce the despised poll tax. Economic conditions were changing, particularly the reduction of inflation to a notably low rate, and unemployment was the lowest it had been for a decade.

Jeremy understood that as with all other consumer goods, the housing market is cyclical. When his intuitive understanding of the nature of markets told him that the property market had reached its peak, he sold. He sold the Lawson property, he sold most of the property contained in his portfolio.

The property boom was disappearing, and the market slumped, not because Jeremy sold, but because Margaret Thatcher's economic party had come to an end and was followed by the inevitable hangover. Overvalued house prices began to drop. When the market was sufficiently depressed Jeremy began to buy once more. He trusted his instincts, and they rarely let him down. He bought houses to redevelop and sell, taking the profit to buy houses to let. He expanded into commercial properties and then small blocks of apartments. He prospered while the overcautious waited.

In the late eighties, financial journalists were blessed with a series of corporate battles that lifted business from its traditional position at the back of newspapers to the front pages: Mohamed Al Fayed's feud with 'Tiny' Rowland over Harrods, Rupert Murdoch's *Sun* pitted against Robert Maxwell's *Mirror*. One name that rarely appeared front or back was Jeremy Lawson's, but that did not mean he was not a serious player.

After the sale of the Queen's Park home, Jeremy needed a suitable place to live. While seeking a replacement at an estate agent's office in St John's Wood, he overheard a conversation at the desk next door. A dejected-looking man was bemoaning his position and ill luck. He had bought a ground-floor apartment in St John's Wood on a 100% mortgage loan and had been servicing the repayments without difficulty until an investment in retail turned sour – a client had reneged on a huge debt, and he was unable to continue to service his mortgage repayments. He was six months overdue, was £50,000 in debt, and the mortgagor was about to foreclose. This would mean not only losing the apartment but his business as well.

Without hesitation Jeremy butted in. "Excuse me, but I couldn't help overhearing your conversation. I have a proposition to put to you." The other man looked at him blankly. The estate agent looked less that impressed. Was his commission about to disappear in front of his eyes?

"What if I offer to repay the £50,000 you owe and pay off the entire mortgage for an additional £450,000?"

"Are you serious?"

"Never more so, and I'll include whatever commission is due."

"Can I think about it?"

"No", said Jeremy as he opened his case and wrote a cheque for £500,000 and another for £10,000 and handed both to the estate agent. Both the vendor and the agent were speechless. Was this really happening? Neither refused. A few moments later, the vendor called his lawyer.

The occurrence was sheer serendipity – as in Monopoly, Jeremy had simply landed on a valuable property - but he had seen its potential and was prepared to take the risk. You may think that to offer five hundred thousand quid for a property he had never seen was bordering on crazy, but Jeremy had explored the area intimately and knew a bargain when it kneeled before him begging on bended knees to be taken.

To the debt-ridden man, this meant he could save his business. Yes, he would wave farewell to a potentially very valuable property, but it was never his to begin with. From Jeremy's perspective, his foresight enabled him to purchase a property that would, on the balance of probabilities, turn out to be worth a lot more.

Five years later he placed it for sale at two million pounds. Two bidders vied against one another, and the property was sold for two million one hundred thousand pounds - four times what he had paid for it. As Jeremy had thought it only worth two million, he transferred £100,000 to the previous owner's bank account. This was a very rare occasion that Jeremy showed goodwill to another.

He loved property markets and economies in poor state when sellers were forced to lower their valuations. Selling the St John's Wood apartment enabled the purchase of a large penthouse suite in Dover Street in Mayfair that he acquired for a knockdown price because the deceased estate was being forced to liquidate in haste. That suite became his residence as well as a gallery not only for his parents' work but included many other rising artists. The value of the Mayfair penthouse and the artwork adorning its walls escalated exponentially - he knew that its current value was little short of fifteen million pounds, excluding the art.

Luxuriously furnished though it had become, the apartment was seen and appreciated by few eyes - the domestic assistant, his chef, his bridge school, an occasional art dealer – one might struggle to name more. Unless it was essential, why would he want to share his hospitality with others? We are talking Jeremy Lawson after all. Scoring a ticket for admission was more difficult than getting a front row seat at La Scala. That was the way Jeremy wanted it and he was content in his seclusion.

Chapter 6

Illegitimi Non Carborundum

"The house you looked at today and wanted to think about until tomorrow may be the same house someone looked at yesterday and will buy today."

The question Jeremy would always ask himself before considering any property venture was, 'What would be the worst possible outcome in a game of chess or bridge?' You get check-mated or fail to make the contract. Thus it was in property - the worst outcome would be to lose on the deal. Loss leads to regret. One therefore had to minimise future regret.

The next question would be, 'What causes loss?' The answer was all too apparent: unmanaged risk. What causes increased risk? Greed. Avoid greed, minimise risk; avoid loss, minimize future regret.

Avoid the error of thinking nothing can go wrong. When things do go wrong, and they often do, it might be due to error on your part or have nothing whatever to do with you, just through chance occurrences. So, what to do when the unwished happens? What is the exit strategy? Jeremy never entered a business deal without having a clear route out should it go toxic.

He understood that dealing in property could be highly competitive, even cut-throat, but he was up for that. More than up for it – he positively enjoyed battle, and the property market proved a perfect battleground. If he had been in the army (an abhorrent thought), he would have been aware of a wartime expression, *illegitimi non carborundum*– don't let the bastards grind you down. Better to be the grinder, and Jeremy did grinding really well.

As he surveyed the scene at the end of the 1980s, he was quick to see that the days when the big banks were in control of London were almost over. The square mile that was known as The City was changing, had changed. Bowler-hatted, umbrella-twirling, plummy-speaking bankers had gone the way of the dodo, often to be replaced by bluff, hard-dealing northerners. Pin-striped ties were replaced by exotic floral, or no ties at all. The era of the property developer had arrived, and they were now running the show. Areas such as Kings Cross and Victoria were ripe for development. Entire council estates were being flattened to make room for residential and commercial properties.

Aristocratic families such as Cadogan, Grosvenor, Portman and the De Waldens who owned Harley Street were being joined by a breed of avaricious corporate giants, national pension funds, and more and more by the untold riches of sovereign international funds and the gushing pump of petrodollars.

As a writer of the day so aptly put it, "We've gone from being ruled by Barclay's Bank to being controlled by Berkeley Homes."

When the banks stopped lending, the London developers turned to investors from the Middle East, Russia and China, fueled by their testosterone-driven dazzling wealth. Money laundering was rife and real estate was the perfect haven for launderers to cleanse ill-gotten gains. At the same time as delivering a reliable and profitable investment, the strategy also provided a veneer of respectability and legitimacy with scrutiny more limited than financial sector transactions.

How was our Jeremy faring in this local-turned-national-turned-international supercharged environment? Far from being fazed, he saw only one word writ large – OPPORTUNITY. He wasn't short of money. He wasn't low on guts. With his legal training and his chess-thinking mind, he was able to apply incisive astuteness in managing the various transactions that accompanied such investments.

Jeremy avoided working with syndicates and partners, something that did not at all suit his lone-wolf mentality. How then was he getting on with people in business? Surprisingly well in many cases. Respected adversaries and enemies were made in equal numbers. Jeremy could be charming, generous and loyal to those who dealt squarely with him. They would always receive a note from him accompanied by a gift from Harrods, or even a car when merited. Was the ugly duckling turning into a swan? Not quite.

On those who crossed him he wreaked vengeance, harbouring titanic-sized grudges, conducting relentless feuds. One of his adversaries was heard to remark, "That guy suffers from 100% pure batshit peevishness!"

Not needing the expense of lawyers, he never hesitated to go to court. He never lost a case. These became fewer with time, as those with whom he dealt would have known in advance that they strayed from ethics and morality at their peril, even if occasionally he did so himself.

He withheld from the temptation to *gazunder.* Although not as upsetting as a transaction withdrawal, gazundering can be a very frustrating occurrence during the selling process. It involves the buyer reducing their offer late in the process, typically prior to the exchange of contracts, leaving the seller to either abandon the sale or take less money. Illegal? No. Unethical, sharp practice? Undoubtedly. Jeremy considered gazundering cheap and nasty.

There was always a distinction that could be discerned in his dealings - the difference between *illegal* and *illicit.* Illicit activities are considered improper or socially forbidden; they may or may not be illegal, but they go against social norms and values. Illegal activities are those that are forbidden by law. Jeremy understood the difference between the two: if you were caught doing something illegal it could mean spending several years at her Majesty's pleasure in a different sort of property. He was never prepared to do anything that would put his freedom at risk.

One of the most intractable of problems for a property developer is a sitting tenant.

Just as in every class of students there is one who will be sure to ask long-winded and inane questions at the end of each lecture, just as on every almost barren plot of land there is one tree that is a protected species and cannot be taken down, so in every building there will be one stubborn individual who refuses to move out, thus halting development. They might be stubborn because they had been born there and intended to die there, or because this was the home where a departed loved one had lived, memories of whom were non-transportable. No matter how much one offered such a person or how luxurious and comfortable the newer premises they were offered might be, they were not going anywhere.

Initially, Jeremy viewed morality only up the point of its own usefulness. Beyond that point, it became a moveable feast. He was quite prepared on occasion to have his morality questioned, at least early on. He was not above using pressure to get sitting tenants to vacate their properties. On the positive side, that pressure never quite included violence and never left the tenant short-changed. Creative solutions would be required - solutions such as placing a rather noisy individual in the vacant apartment next door with a passion for heavy-metal music played at high decibels all hours of the day and night but especially at 4am. Complaints to the police might result in a visit and a warning, but simple replacement of one music lover by another with a need to practise playing a trumpet throughout the day meant the issue was not going to depart before the sitting tenant did. The obstinate tenant would later be found living in a newer, far smarter apartment nearby thinking nostalgically about what used to be. Unethical, sharp practice? Undoubtedly. When necessity compels, needs must when the devil drives.

Looking back on these tactics years later when he was much richer and a little kinder, Jeremy would wince, but attributed it to the exuberance of youth. However, he was not by nature rapacious, and soon began to forego these unsavoury tactics and the reputation that accompanied such practice. He relied on understanding the market rather than on guile and cunning.

There could be no doubt that Jeremy was well up on a ladder and climbing steadily upwards. By the time he reached the age of forty at the turn of the century, he was an acknowledged presence in the world of property. He had been exploited on occasion, but on many, many more he had been the exploiter. There were many people who disliked him for what they perceived was a ruthless drive for wealth, but even they held a grudging respect.

Indulging in niceties was not part of Jeremy's armamentarium, certainly not at that time. One short article on page 33 of The Times described him as "Having the mindset of a North Korean border guard but without the charm; despite always being immaculately attired and of impeccable manners, he was never more than icy cold with a whiff of menace." A bit extreme, you might say ...

After one territorial tussle with a far more experienced developer for a small block of offices and shops that had the potential to become a large one, Jeremy emerged with the title deeds in his briefcase. He overheard the developer muttering to his lawyers, "That motherfucker is like a demented warlord – attack, attack, attack. Thinks he's Winston bloody Churchill. Never seen anything like it."

I'll take that, thought Jeremy, perhaps a bit smugly.

Was Jeremy a misanthrope? Did he really dislike all humankind? Let's do a checklist:

Did he lack desire to participate in social activities of any kind? Tick.

Did he feel indifference or even aversion toward emotional things that most people feel in human connection? Tick.

Was there a tendency to be less emotional and more practical than most people? Tick.

Was there rudeness and bluntness in conversation? The jury is out, but let's give him the benefit of the doubt on this one.

What is abundantly clear is that Jeremy did have an antisocial personality. As a counterargument, it should also be mentioned that several charities were benefitting substantially from his largesse. This enigma is not easily explained given that he seemed to dislike or mistrust most of the people with whom he had contact, almost all of whom shared one thing with him: privilege. On the other hand, there were a lot more people on the planet who for whatever reason had found themselves outsiders: the disabled, the poor, the unfortunate. Being a stoic outsider himself, he identified marginally with them and felt a slight degree of sympathy. So, giving to the needy seemed a decent thing to do, especially as it was tax-deductible.

Chapter 7
The Scheissters

** The shitheads, from the vulgar German word Scheisse (excrement), hence "scheisster", also spelled shyster, is a slang word for someone who acts in a disreputable, unethical or unscrupulous way.*

"Real estate cannot be lost or stolen, nor can it be carried away. Purchased with common sense, paid for in full, and managed with reasonable care, it is about the safest investment in the world." - Franklin D. Roosevelt

Roosevelt was not always correct. On a couple of occasion in the mid-nineties, Jeremy Lawson came very close to losing a lot of money in property scams. It was a time when property fraud was rife. Was it possible for a scammer to sell a house they did not own? Unfortunately, yes.

Criminal scheissters were actively selling properties by impersonating owners using false or stolen ID. They often targeted sole, absent or deceased owners. False companies, fake conveyancers, identity theft: these were the stock-in-trade for the less than honest who were invading the field.

Some years before, Jeremy Lawson had bought a delightful property in Hampshire that he used as a weekend bolthole. A man named Sowerby lived in a delightful-looking home nearby, but the two men were not acquainted. Not entirely unusual in the south of England you might say, where people do not often know their neighbours, but we are speaking here of two absentee homeowners.

Jeremy was rather surprised when he received a letter from a legal firm informing him that Mr Sowerby wanted to sell and was offering him first option. The price mentioned seemed surprisingly reasonable and the property would make a solid investment. Jeremy instructed his solicitor to nail the deal and authorised payment of £75,000 as a deposit, duly carried out.

Matters seemed to be progressing satisfactorily and far quicker than one would have expected. Then the *scheisse* hit the fan.

While away from his property, Sowerby was tipped off by another neighbour that a stranger was seen entering his home. He went there to find the locks had been changed. He was shocked to find a man occupying the premises who had paid full market value for a property that Sowerby (the real owner) had not sold and certainly not to him. It transpired that Sowerby's identity had been stolen and used to sell the house, and the fraudsters were able to bank the proceeds.

The legitimate owner, Sowerby, immediately contacted the police and was shocked when told by the officer that they didn't believe a criminal offence had been committed - this was a civil matter and there was nothing further they could do. His inability to get police support for the issue shocked him.
On investigation, it turned out that the renewal form for his driving licence issued by the Licensing Agency had been stolen; his identity was stolen with it. The crooks used spoof solicitor letterheads to request payment, and a bank account had been set up in Sowerby's name, the proceeds of the sale received by electronic transfer. The legal firm involved for the purported vendor was of course entirely bogus. The buyer was scammed into handing over £750,000 and the legitimate owner had lost his home. Or had he? A massive dispute was ensuing about who was now the legitimate owner.

It transpired that the greedy fraudsters had sold the house once already and saw no reason why they should not be reselling it a second time to Jeremy. All things considered, one supposes that Jeremy should have been grateful that he only lost £75,000! To Jeremy, however, it mattered little whether the amount was £7,500 or £75,000. What mattered was that he had been done, and did not like being done. What could he do about it? Nothing but learn. That was the most bitter pill of all.

The second issue concerned one of the properties that Aida Property Holdings had purchased early on, a delightful garden flat in a new-build apartment block in Maida Vale. It had an all-glass frontage looking onto a Japanese-styled garden and the canal beyond. The apartment was a sun trap – one did not need to put on the heating, even on a cold day. The flat was in mint condition and Jeremy had considered occupying it himself but decided to let it and wait for a few years for the flat to appreciate.

The letting agent, Rashid, had found three very charming tenants in succession, the first an attractive Italian tv actress, followed by a couple of newlyweds from Hong Kong and then a budding author from Glasgow who'd just tied up a neat contract for his first book.

When the writer's lease was about to terminate, Jeremy contacted Rashid, and within days, a meeting had been set up with a prospective tenant who came from Abu Dhabi. The immaculately dressed young man requested a two-year lease, and to Jeremy's surprise asked if he could pay in four instalments, the first six months in advance. Jeremy wasn't about to say no, especially when, after due diligence, the references seemed cast-iron.

Six months later, Jeremy was on a business mission in the USA when he received a message from Rashid asking him to call.

"Hello, Rashid, you asked me to phone you - is there a problem?"

"I'm afraid so, Mr Lawson – the cheque for the second instalment has bounced. I've emailed Mr Al Tahir and he's responded, saying he's having problems with his bank in Abu Dhabi, and he's gone back to sort it out. He says not to worry, it will be settled soon."

"Ok, let it run, but keep in touch."

The next day he received a call from Molly, the manager of the company responsible for maintenance of the building.

"Hi Mr Lawson, I've just received a phone call from the young woman now occupying the flat. You didn't tell me there was a new tenant. Has Mr Al Tahir sublet or something?"

"Well, if he has, he's in breach of his lease. I know nothing about this, Molly."

"Anyway, she's requesting a key for the tenant's mailbox in the hall. She's also complained that the cleaners of the flat have stolen her jewellery box worth a thousand pounds, and she's saying they are nothing but a pair of Bulgarian prostitutes. This really upsets me, Mr Lawson - they've worked for me for years and I've never had a previous complaint."

"Don't give her any keys. Something weird is going on, but I'll check it out when I return in a week's time."

Before he could do so, he received an email from Molly. She was concerned because she was receiving phone calls from several other apartment owners about the new tenant smoking in the passages and stubbing out her cigarettes on the wall. The passage was smelling like an ashtray, and the smell was permeating through to their apartments. Mrs Thomas in flat 10 had also complained, saying the new tenant was parking her car in Mrs Thomas's reserved space.

Molly copied an email she had just opened.

Hi there, this is Davide from Nexus Court Building in Malvern Road.

I'm writing to let you know that the tenants of flat number 3 are doing too much noise every single night. Right now, 1:40 in the night, the girl was ringing repeatedly our doorbell, and when we opened the door she just said that was a mistake. Considering that me and my girlfriend work every day this situation is becoming very stressful for us, also last week the floor was full of people in her flat with much smoke, also the other type of cigarettes. So please, if you can, try to do something as soon as possible.

Jeremy was extremely perturbed. Female, smoking in the hallway? Marijuana? Noisy late-night parties? This woman was clearly the proverbial trespasser from hell.

On his return, he took a taxi to Maida Vale, let himself into the building with his spare key, and the first thing he noticed was that the mailbox had been forced open. He knocked on the door of no.3. After a delay, the door was partially opened and a red-eyed, rather large, rather stoned young woman in a dressing-gown peered out, cigarette in hand. Her pencil-thin, just-visible moustache was the same colour as the matted black mass of hair on her head, fortunately less copious. And then there was the hair on her legs.

"Yes?" said the Medusa, in a voice sounding as if it required passing through a sieve.

Jeremy involuntarily stepped backwards, then with composure regained, said, "I'm the owner of this flat, and I'd like to know what you are doing in it."

"You're not the owner. It's Mr Al Tahir's, and he's in Abu Dhabi. I'm also from there and I've paid him two years' rent in advance, so fuck off."

Jeremy had taken the precaution of bringing a copy of the lease with him, but as he attempted to show it to her, she slammed the door in his face. He knocked again. This time the door was opened by an unsavoury-looking foreign man who had obviously neither shaved nor showered in days. He reeked of ashtray and sweat.

The man, clearly under the influence of something noxious, politely managed to mumble, "You get fuck out of here ok or I call police!"

Jeremy was now approaching boiling point. He somehow managed to control himself and respond, "No, it is I who'll be calling the police. You are trespassing illegally in my flat," before he stormed off.

The police of course were not at all interested. After another couple of attempts to gain entry to no avail, by which time the amount allegedly stolen by the cleaners had risen to three thousand pounds, Jeremy knew he had a big problem, a problem that might only be sorted out in a court of law. He knew it would take many months to gain an eviction order. Getting a couple of thugs to move her out was unfortunately not a viable solution either.

Rashid tried to contact Al Tahir – no response. Then he tried the referees – no response either. Bogus? For sure.

Jeremy went back to the flat, and on this occasion she was not stoned, but was rather abusive. She still would not allow him into the apartment and came out to the passage with her own 'lease' as granted by Al Tahir. Her name was Yousa, and she too was from Abu Dhabi. Yousa had paid him a year's rent in advance, £24,000, four times what he was to have paid Jeremy. Where do people get that kind of money? Of course - Abu Dhabi! This discussion was repeated several times and Jeremy realised he was not going to sort out this mess easily.

Yousa the Medusa eventually realised she had been taken for a ride, and agreed to move out if Jeremy would refund her the £24,000 plus £3,000 to fund the removal of her goods (which turned out to be just four suitcases-worth) to another flat. Realising how much time he would have to waste on this sordid affair and get nothing back for it if he did not accept Yousa's terms, he grudgingly agreed. The final straw was when she demanded that the money be paid *before* she moved out, but the look on Jeremy's face and his suggestion that if she wasn't gone within forty-eight hours she might need to leave by ambulance was enough to convince her that pushing him any further was not a good idea.

What a debacle! Together with the four months it had taken with rent unpaid, plus the cost of refurbishing the damage caused within – before leaving, they had trashed the place and ripped up the furniture and blinds - Jeremy was out of pocket by the mere matter of £38,000. Not that it was going to bankrupt him, but it was another expensive lesson. What really irked Jeremy, though, was that the oleaginous Mr Al Tahir had pocketed a clear £18,000 profit and there was nothing Jeremy could do about it.

Chapter 8

Opportunities

You want to predict the future? Difficult. What most do is to remove finger from mouth and hold up to air. Occasionally it points in the right direction. Better to be awake to the world around. Timing is everything. Availability of mortgages, prevailing economic and international disasters can wreak havoc on the market. Look at the effects of Brexit, Covid and Ukraine today. And especially bad government.

Ever aware of market trends, Jeremy began to take a strong interest in the increasing involvement of wealthy families buying properties abroad to use as holiday homes. Why have your children mooch around playing on their iPads at home or at a washed-out seaside resort in rainy England, when, for the same price as a small apartment in the UK, you could rent or even buy an apartment or a house in countries like Spain and more recently in Croatia and South Africa - especially if there was a favorable monetary exchange rate to make the price gap even more attractive.

Once more Jeremy had to make a call on whether the obvious bandwagon would be able to be ridden *before* it disappeared from sight. He decided this was a burgeoning business opportunity, a lodestone to be seized and squeezed. Jeremy's company began to buy run-down properties - apartments, houses, buildings - in seaside towns abroad and renovate them before letting them or reselling. Aida Investments quickly built up a decent portfolio of properties on mainland Europe, and once again the venture was proving lucrative.

Jeremy then began to diversify his portfolio of investments, a little more conservatively this time, re-investing his already sizeable fortune in very safe stocks and bonds that were not only growing steadily but were providing him with a wonderfully luxurious and opulent lifestyle. Simultaneously, Jeremy had become both a warrior and a *bon vivant* and used the talents required for the former to fund the latter. He never hesitated to spend lavishly on travel, music, art and especially on perfectly prepared food by imaginative chefs.

'Franchise' was the new buzzword, making it possible for the small man to get into the big business act. Tie Rack, Sock Shop, Bodyshop, everywhere you looked. Costa Coffee too. Coffee was the new tea. One could make vast sums by selling stuff – but even better and with much less hard work was owning the properties where the stuff was being sold.

Much as he had loathed football as a child, he saw the value of acquiring hospitality boxes at Arsenal, Spurs and Chelsea, not for his own pleasure but for that of the wheeler-dealers who would be his guests, and they proved to be brilliant investments. Once the copious flow of proffered champagne, wine and whisky had loosened the tongues of his wealthy guests, he was able to find out what those dealers were involved with in the market. Forewarned was forearmed.

Not every business deal had a pleasant odour, and many simply stank of ordure. Something that did not stink, not to Jeremy's nose at any rate, was the powerful aroma to be found in Scotch whisky. Over the years, he had developed a passionate interest in single malts. This began, strangely enough, after a visit not to Scotland but to Australia where he had been introduced to a 20-year-old medal-winning Tasmanian single malt. Once that molten liquid bug bit, it didn't easily let go.

This minibeast had led to countless trips to the mother country distilleries in the Highlands, Speyside, and the Isles of Skye and Jura. Jeremy bought a small but very exclusive new distillery on Skye to which he would repair whenever opportunity presented. The distillery was in its adolescent growth stage, with the nascent spirit maturing nicely in ancient casks. All the predictions pointed to a peaty whisky that would challenge the likes of Talisker, no mean compliment. Jeremy may have loved his wine with great passion, but he was a firm believer that there was no wine that would not be improved by being book-ended with a hearty peat whisky to start and a sherry-, port- or brandy-casked whisky to bring a meal to conclusion. As he explained to his chief distiller, "Some whiskies want to get you drunk, some want to challenge you. What I'm looking for is a premium single malt that really wants to take you to dinner."

His man looked Jeremy in the eye and said, "Dinner it shall be, Mr Lawson, at Le Gavroche - I'm sure Mr Roux would be happy to share a wee dram of our best!"

Jeremy Lawson had cause to be happy with his assets. Never once did he consider that he might wish to share his wealth with a life-partner either male or female, and marriage was the furthest thing from his mind. In fact, he found the whole notion of having physical contact with another human rather repulsive - there were better ways to screw them. Holden Caulfield, eat your heart out ...

Chapter 9

Daniel Odenfemji

Having worked with great vision and commendable focus on acquiring his wealth, Jeremy was not about to give it away easily. Never taking chances unduly, he checked every word in each bit of paperwork, and then checked again. Everything in Jeremy's world was based on careful risk evaluation. Where others saw property and buildings, Jeremy saw statistics and probabilities. If the odds showed that it was more likely than not for the deal to have a favourable outcome, he placed a bet. Where a positive outcome seemed unlikely, even if only slightly, he turned away. You had to be prepared to sacrifice pawns, even bishops or knights, but you never put your king at risk.

The surest way to put your king in the firing line is to attract the attention of an organisation that felt entitled to your money as much as you do – Inland Revenue. Jeremy regarded Inland Revenue (the opposition's queen) as a necessary evil, but one whose demands could be limited with careful planning. Avoid the raising of red flags in the cramped tax offices of the north. Pre-empt suspicion. Avoid investigation. With an ability to craft his business accounts creatively, figures could be made to conjure any outcome desired. Rely rather on alchemy, endow spreadsheets with figures able to cast bewitching spells on lesser minds. Nullify that queen, protect your king.

One of the very few occasions that Jeremy strayed from his low-risk policy was a property investment deal in which he got involved with a Nigerian named Daniel Odenfemji. He had been introduced to Mr Odenfemji by a director of Churchhaven, where Jeremy banked. The banker was himself of very respectable reputation, although Jeremy was later to learn that the glitzy cover of that book did not reflect the untrustworthy character that lurked within, Eton or not.

Another of the bank's clients who was involved in the property project was a cabinet minister of impeccable provenance – as rare as rocking-horse poop these days - and this provided the comfort blanket that persuaded Jeremy to become involved in the deal that became known as the Brandenberg Project (Vivaldi's masterpiece was the last concert the banker had attended.)

Daniel Odenfemji was an extremely charming gentleman and well-spoken, as one would expect from someone who had been educated at Marlborough UK, Columbia (New York) and an MBA from Wharton Business School. It is well known that one has to have at least five million in assets to have an account at Churchhaven, and Mr Odenfemij had easily qualified on that score and had passed the scrutiny of the Churchhaven auditors on the strength of the testimonials of his nominees.

Daniel Odenfemji owned a 16-storey high-rise business building that stood out as the most modern edifice in Lagos, the city of his birth. His residence occupied the top two floors, but he spent little time there. In addition to this, Odenfemji owned property in several other big cities including London, New York, and most luxurious of all, an apartment in Milan. He tended to return to Lagos only occasionally.

Mr Odenfemji had been seeking someone who would be a safe pair of hands for an enormous sum of money that he was bringing through from his home city, and Jeremy fitted that bill perfectly. No, this wasn't one of those toxic e-mail scams that all of us have received at some time or another - the Brandenburg Project was for real. Jeremy's role was to be the nominal purchaser of a very large office block in east London for an amount that ran into eight figures and close to nine. Jeremy was not required to make any financial investment himself. However, he would be expected to resell the property within a few months to a consortium registered in Dubai.

Money laundering was rife, not least from Vladimir Putin via his Russian cronies, and real estate was the perfect haven for money launderers to cleanse ill-gotten gains. Residential and commercial properties, at the same time as delivering a reliable and profitable investment strategy also provided a veneer of respectability, legitimacy and normality, with scrutiny more limited than financial sector transactions.

Real estate money-laundering was a complex process. Intricate loans and credit finance often had to be arranged, not always with ease. Manipulation of the valuation of a property was a big part of the deal - sometimes they had to be under-valued, at others over-appraised. The one constant was concealment of ownership, and for that, recourse to third parties and use of front companies and trusts were essential.

Jeremy, not being thick, realised from the off that what he was being offered by his bankers was nothing more or less than a money-laundering operation. You had to be blind not to realise that this was dry-cleaning on a large scale, but it suited most people in the banks and financial services to ignore such trivial details completely. Jeremy's first instinct was to turn down the offer out of hand, but this one seemed rock-solid. Most out of character for a person who was as risk averse as Jeremy, he decided to proceed on the yellow signal – with caution. Although money-laundering had not yet become labelled as a crime against humanity, it was the kind of activity that would bring an individual or organisation under intensive scrutiny. Being tainted as a launderer would be an unwelcome stain on one's reputation if it went awry.

It did not go awry. Both deals, the initial purchase and subsequent resale, went through without a hitch, and Jeremy realised an after-tax profit in excess of one million, five hundred thousand pounds when his involvement terminated. Not a bad return for eleven months of not very hard labour that involved little more work than a couple of signatures!

Incidentally, the Churchhaven banker was arrested a few years later for allegedly helping to launder at least 5 billion yen linked to a large Japanese yakuza gang. His defence that he was 'unaware' of the source of the money did not sit well with the jury, and the banker ended up sitting not well in a small room in HMP Wandsworth. That was until he was found dead in his cell from a suspected heart attack. The Brandenberg project never came to light.

The most unusual thing about the whole deal was that, probably for the first time ever, Jeremy had found a person with whom he enjoyed working, who shared and (more important) respected his interests in opera and fine food. The Brandenburg Project business transaction did not prove the end of their association at a social level. Jeremy sensed that Daniel was not a fly-by-night investor – he was urbane, sophisticated, a connoisseur of the Arts, and had impeccable taste in dining. They began to communicate more frequently, and for his part Daniel was grateful that this older man was proving to be a fount of wisdom in guiding him through other non-laundering deals and helping him to avoid the pitfalls that were peculiar to English business dealings and ethics.

Jeremy received and accepted occasional invitations from Daniel Odenfemji to attend evenings at the jewel in the operatic crown that was La Scala in Milan. That wasn't all. There were also dinners at Enrico Bartolini's two-Michelin-starred haute cuisine restaurant inside Milan's avant-garde Mudec museum, a privilege granted to few, and cruises with Daniel and his lovely wife on nearby Lake Maggiore on Daniel's luxurious cabin cruiser. All in all, a win-win relationship. It did not take long for

Jeremy to realise that, perhaps for the first time in his life, he had met a soul-partner, twenty years younger than he.

Daniel had been born with a silver spoon in his mouth. No, more than a spoon. An entire cutlery set. Having a mouthful of cutlery, whether silver, gold or stainless steel, could have had the effect of choking a young man had his head not been properly screwed on – but Daniel's was, and as Jeremy was later to discover, this was extremely surprising. It was some time after the deal had been concluded that Jeremy became privy to the fact that a long while back, Daniel had changed his name from his birth surname, Alewaju, taking on his mother's maiden name, Odenfemji.

The reason for this change was that the father of Jeremy's erstwhile trading partner in the Brandenburg Project was a notorious crime baron in Lagos who was indeed involved in massive money laundering operations, and the project that Jeremy, Daniel, Churchhaven and the cabinet minister had shared was providing the transport vehicle for a large part of the senior Nigerian's ill-gotten fortune.

Nigerian criminal gangs had risen to unwanted prominence during the eighties. Their activities included fraud, looting and kidnappings. According to the FBI, Nigerian criminal enterprises were the most notable of all ventures of that ilk. They were considered to be among the most aggressive international criminal groups, operating in more than 80 countries worldwide. Their most profitable activity was drug trafficking, though they were more famous for their financial fraud which was costing the US alone approximately 2 billion dollars annually.

Daniel's father, Abimbola Alewaju was a very rich man in what was generally a very poor country. He was known to be an arrogant and self-important person and a notorious womaniser. He was not without enemies - other barons whose turf he had crossed were an on-going threat. At least three attempts of which he was aware had been made on his life. Six bodyguards and two chauffeurs had been blown up or shot, but he had somehow survived and prospered.

It had been said that money is only dirty when laundered, but laundering money was far from the most heinous crime in which Mr Alewaju involved himself - it just happened to be the end product. It was alleged that Mr Alewaju Snr was one of several gangsters from his country who had made massive money through dubious international channels such as the sale of fake and dangerous drugs and sophisticated fraudulent scams. In their infamous empires, they were the linchpins: dangerous, merciless, cynical and destructive in their operations. They held the key to life and death of many people through their nefarious enterprises. They were a small minority of the population, yet their bite was enough to taint Nigeria as a country to be regarded with utmost suspicion.

When Abimbola Alewaju was arrested in the UK at some point following a massive swindle, he told the anti-fraud security men, "Don't waste your time, gentlemen. I am a veteran in these cases. I have been dealing with the police for many years." Was he alluding to a corrupt element within the fraud squad that was amenable to bribery? Or were there threats against the well-being of those law officers and their families? Probably both. Despite what seemed an irrefutable case against him, witnesses had either not turned up or had amended their statements, and Abimbola Alewaju walked from the Old Bailey a free man. He did not resent the massive legal fees he had to pay his solicitors and barrister and a number of witnesses, because in the scheme of things, it was a pittance.

Although it was his father's money that had paid for Daniel's expensive education, Daniel was sufficiently competent and savvy to amass a fortune on his own account. Although not on bad terms with his father, Daniel was a man cut from much finer cloth. A great deal less dishonest than his father, he chose to have as little as possible to do with him business-wise. Did Daniel feel good about abetting his father? No, but like Michael Corleone, he was unable to dissociate completely from his origins. He hoped fervently that the financial benefits gained through the Brandenburg Project would enable him to keep those ties as tenuous as possible, if not severing them completely.

Fortunately for the son, no aspersions were ever cast on Daniel's good name. Or for that matter on Jeremy's. Nevertheless, Jeremy resolved after that not to put himself, his reputation or his assets at risk ever again. He did however have cause later to be extremely grateful to have made the acquaintance of this handsome and cultured African.

Chapter 10

Spanish Clouds

"John Constable painted clouds to study their shape and anatomy. Rene Magritte's cloud paintings invited the viewer to free their mind from all prejudice and thought."

Up to this point, Jeremy's Spanish portfolio had served him well. Unfortunately, he was about to receive a lesson in clouds. Not about cirrus, cumulus, nimbus and stratus. Not about fine art. Not even data-storing clouds. He would learn there were three other types of clouds: clouds with silver linings, dark clouds, and black clouds. He would learn that every silver lining has a nasty habit of being associated with a dark cloud, and dark clouds could turn black.

Squatting is a dark cloud. It has a long history in Spain, often fueled by high rates of homelessness. With the massive influx of refugees from Africa, a property that was unoccupied for even a short period was at risk of being taken over by squatters. In some instances, the squatters would change the locks of empty apartments, then sell the keys for many euros to impoverished people struggling to pay a market rent. This would then serve as a home for many more people that ever intended. One might have a certain degree of sympathy for the needy, but getting them out of a property that one owned could be a longwinded and expensive legal process.

Unfortunately for Aida Property Holdings, there was another, much darker variety of cloud - squatters who were professional extortionists, often from Eastern Europe or the Middle East, demanding a ransom before they would vacate a property. This trend was beginning to impact rather badly on the lawful activities of Jeremy's company. Initially, he tried to deal with the issue through the law. Trespassers would be reported to the police, who would take the case to a judge. Unfortunately, as Jeremy was beginning to learn, it might take up to two years for the courts to make a decision and it would not always go the way of an absentee landlord especially if the landlord was a *gringo.*

If the occupants were easily attracted by the opportunity of making quick money that was easier than robbing a bank, then terms would be arranged with the owner and the squatters would leave and find accommodation elsewhere, sometimes even next-door. If not, stronger tactics were required.

Jeremy received an unwelcome phone call from his agent in Barcelona.

"Senor Hereme, I ham sorry for say but in house in Roses is *okupas.* I go there and I see is four of them. They are playing the cards on the *patio de aasa*. I say *vamanos, amigos,* and they say for me they are wanting 5,000 euros to leave. What I must do, Senor Hereme?"

What to do? What were his options? Jeremy could go the legal route, the high road. Or he could negotiate with the squatters to get them out. Or he could hire one of a burgeoning number of private eviction companies that used threats (and if that didn't work, violence) to achieve their goal. Taking the high road - the route through the courts - was not to be considered. As for the other two options Jeremy was not averse to either. He decided that, in the first instance, he would negotiate, despite it rewarding crooks for their bad conduct and conflicting with his abhorrence of allowing criminals to profit.

If the uninvited tenants proved obdurate and negotiation failed to bring a reasonable result at a reasonable price, well then, the hard men would have to be called in. There were firms who employed ex-boxers and martial Arts experts. Jeremy had on occasion resorted to using such odious methods. He found this very distasteful, because a bit more than a conversation usually ensued, and people were known to get hurt: a broken finger or two, a fractured arm, re-arranged kneecaps. Nothing terribly serious, but a nuisance for all on the wrong end of a hammer or a pair of pliers.

So the game would begin. He authorized Jose to negotiate.

Jose called back. "Hereme, I able to make the figure down to 2,000 euros."

'Hereme' didn't hesitate. "Just pay it", he said.

So the money was paid, but did the uninvited tenants move out? Not a chance. They said they were going nowhere, not until they received the balance owing of 3,000 euros. What they received was an extremely thorough beating from persons unknown. Then they limped rather than walked from the property.

And then came other black clouds - the blackmailers.

Another day, another call. Jeremy received a phone call in London from someone with a thick European accent: "Hey Mister, the house you own in Costa Brava, you know which one. I send you pictures if you like. I have break into this place, I'm in your house. Hey Mister, I going to destroy it. You want me no destroy, you transferring money to my account."

"What's your price?"

"Ten thousand dollar US."

"Are you loco?! I can get any damage you do repaired for less than that."

"Mister, when I'm finis, that is cost plenty! Is will be nothing left to repair."

Jeremy realised he needed to buy time. "Whoa - we're sending someone to see you to discuss the situation."

"Non possible. You pay now."

"Ok, ok. Money will be delivered in three days."

"Tomorrow."

"Not possible. It will require a foreign bank transfer. It's complicated."

"Ok, so listen Mister, if money no transfer in tree day, I make hole in every pipe in house. I pull every wire from wall, make pasta. Fires. You understand me, Senor Mister, I no jokin."

Jeremy didn't think he was.

Newton's First Law of motion states that if a body is at rest it will remain at rest unless it acted upon by a force. Newton's Third Law of motion states that when two forces interact there is an equal and opposite reaction. The force had acted, and Jeremy was compelled to react. Jeremy did what he was beginning to do more and more frequently - he consulted with his new best friend (probably his only real friend).

"Daniel? Jeremy."

"Hi bro, how's it going?"

"You know my property in Roses?" (he used the Spanish pronunciation, *Roshas*) "Just got a phone call from my manager there. I have a squatter."

"Ok, so what's the problem?"

"He's threatening to deconstruct the place."

"How much does he want to leave it constructed?"

"$10,000. My first thought was to negotiate with him."

"What was your second thought?"

"To send someone with muscles to have a chat with him."

"I like your second thought more. I'll call you back."

Within the hour, Jeremy's cell phone buzzed.

Daniel's handsome face on the screen, his calming voice. "My dad has a couple of friends in France at the moment. It will take them a day to get there. They can be very persuasive. The bad news is that they charge for flexing their muscles. Three grand each. Would you like me to have a friendly chat with them?"

"Go."

Two days later, Mr Abimbola Alewaju's colleagues sent photos of a stranger with an arm at a very strange angle. That was for *hors d'oeuvres.* For the main course, a couple of missing knuckles served on a white plate with blood-coloured gravy, followed by a photo of eyes that would not be seeing much for a while, served as dessert. A creative cuisine. On second thoughts, destructive might be a more suitable adjective.

Yes, it had cost Jeremy six thousand dollars, but at least the money had been honestly earned.

Jeremy realised it was time to reconsider whether this foreign investment game was worth the candle, decided it was not, and began to divest.

Chapter 11

Sanguivorous?

Jeremy Lawson had acquired a reputation as a hard dealer, but even he was taken by surprise when a reporter for a provincial financial newspaper wrote a rather scurrilous article about him.

He described Jeremy as "*...being fair up to the point of being slighted. If, however, you get on the wrong side of Jeremy Lawson, he has the reputation of a man who does not easily forget nor quickly forgive. The man is clearly sanguivorous – enjoying the taste of blood, especially that of another human. This makes one think that his birthplace might well have been Transylvania.*

The best thing that anyone can say about him is that he is morally and ethically blank. His selfishness, cynicism and sneering take on the business world encapsulates everything wrong with the entire generation of men who are currently devouring the world with their unabandoned gluttony.

Not that he needed it, but Jeremy Lawson then began to sell his knowledge for obscene amounts of money, running courses on property investment and trading on the name of his alma mater, the London Business School. Many people invested up to £20,000 for a course on how to make money from property. How could they possibly go wrong? Well, unfortunately they did after Mr Lawson summarily pulled the plug on the programme and failed to reimburse his students. Mr Lawson did not seem to care a great deal when that project failed lamentably. As he was heard to comment, "So their gamble didn't come off – tough!"

You can trust a dog to guard your house, but never trust a dog to guard your sandwich, and I would not let a certain person anywhere near my lunch pack.

Clearly then, not a man to be trifled with.

The reporter was correct about the last sentiment – he was later made to regret his choice of words when he was sued for defamation. Jeremy conducted his own legal case. Why the reporter was so scathing in his condemnation of Jeremy never came out in court, and the reporter was unable to produce a scintilla of evidence of any kind to back his insulting assertions. When the defendant's barrister asked Lawson why he had failed to complete the property courses, Jeremy responded that he never run such courses – he said his estimation of mankind was insufficient to want to share his hard-earned wisdom, he didn't need the money, and that the person who did was someone with a similar-sounding name cashing in.

Jeremy rarely disagreed with the notion that the law was an ass, but in this case he was able to turn it into a sleek stallion. The judge found for him and awarded substantial damages that Jeremy promptly donated to Battersea Dogs' Home. Even though they could not be trusted to guard sandwiches, Jeremy generally preferred dogs to people. Not that he loved dogs greatly either.

The reporter never wrote another article, and the newspaper folded.

It was not that the reporter's assessment of the mogul was entirely without foundation. What Jeremy was doing was not much different from others in the game, only he did it with greater aplomb and a lot more finesse, and even if he drained their marrow, he never drank anyone's blood.

Chapter 12
La Dolce Vita

All this notwithstanding, forty-year-old Jeremy had mellowed considerably over the years. At the turn of the century, his antipathy to other humans had substantially if not completely diminished. No longer did he see himself as the Howard Roark of his generation, in fact quite the opposite. Being involved in the world of property, he could not avoid constant contact with others, nor did he wish to. He was even known to smile occasionally. He had several male acquaintances whose company he enjoyed when the occasion suited, who equally enjoyed his, and who valued his advice on matters financial (but never attended courses).

He had reached that point in his working life where he was not just different from everyone except the super-rich by having 'more money', but that the making of more money had ceased to have meaning to him other than figures on a bank statement. Far from enjoying jousting with others of his ilk who boasted about who could earn more or spend more or buy bigger yachts, he preferred to keep a very low profile. He was in the habit of regularly donating large sums to various charities, but few knew of this.

He was also playing a serious and keen game of bridge on three or four evenings a week and was much sought after as a partner in tournaments. And then of course there were the opera and ballet afficionados with whom he regularly conversed, in particular his doctor, Victor Smythe, who was the source of many stories about divas and diletantes.

He had some female acquaintances too, all of the same generation as Jeremy and married to his business and bridge associates. Terming any of them 'friends' would be stretching the elastic a shade too far - little Sophie's legacy still ruled. His financial and bridge colleagues never felt threatened when their wives elected to accept the invitations that were of no interest to the clients themselves, for example an evening at the Royal Ballet at Covent Garden. On the contrary, the suits were only too pleased to see their spouses go off for a very expensive evening that would cost them not a penny; an evening that would enable the suits to have a free night to watch football or to spend time doing what they knew with absolute certainty their wives would not be doing.

Their presence helped his business needs because they were only too happy to chat about their husbands' business activities. A thoroughly pleasant evening would be spent by Jeremy with such ladies in his private box at the Royal Opera House where his personal valet served canapes and champagne, blinis and caviar. Never once did it cross Jeremy's mind to as much as hold a hand; a hand that might have been very readily given, because when a man has a pile of money, that can often be a powerful aphrodisiac.

If anyone was foolish enough to broach the subject of his lack of marital attachment, perhaps with the intention of setting him up with a lonesome friend, Jeremy would snap back that he had spent his entire life to that point celibate and single and had no intention of altering the status quo. He was not broken, he would add, ergo there was nothing that required fixing.

A confirmed Europhile, Jeremy's zest for the good life stretched all over the continent. He was passionate about Russian ballet, Italian opera, Danish cuisine, French wine, Swedish furniture and British art. If one is passionate about anything, the most useful asset to indulging that lust is to have sufficient resources to be able to afford as much of the object as one would wish to have. Jeremy wished much but never in excess, and was certainly able to afford whatever he wanted.

He wished to have a wine cellar, so he converted the basement of a property in Camden. Temperature and humidity were maintained by an elaborate climate control system to reduce temperature swing. After the conversion was completed, Jeremy was an ever-present figure at wine auctions at Sotheby's, Christie's, Bonham's, Bacchus and several other specialist venues. Buying, but also on occasion selling. Over a matter of ten years, he had stocked his cellar with more vintage Premier Grand Cru and the best from the New World vineyards than he could drink in a lifetime, even though he was trying his best to do so.

Four thousand bottles are a lot to get through, so there was more than enough for others. Presenting a bottle of Chateau Margaux when a deal had been concluded or when invited out for dinner or before a game of bridge did nothing to diminish his status nor his appreciation by others. Not so sanguivorous after all.

THE LONDON FINANCIAL GAZETTE

Who is Jeremy Lawson?

Wed 26 March 2004

Opulence has been manifested differently over the ages, some societies more than others. From the ancient Roman property scammer-turned-general Marcus Licinius Crassus, via Cosimo di Medici and renaissance Florence to the conquistadores and the great American tycoons, the same impulses emerge - for wealth to be in plain sight. Display of one's wealth was to be ogled at, desired and envied. Better to be of the have-yachts than the have-nots.

Time changes. What do multimillionaires / billionaires look like these days? Do they wear heavy gold necklaces and uber-cool shades, sweaters with big-brand logos? Probably not. The one thing this breed seeks today, that they have difficulty in finding, is seclusion. Seclusion from their critics, seclusion from the press, seclusion even from their friends unless a deal is involved. They prefer low profile to bling.

Even from his earliest days when Jeremy Lawson became wealthy, he has never had to seek seclusion - anonymity has stuck to him like the pluck of a sheep to the skin of a haggis. He may be a super-rich property wheeler-dealer, but he is a man who likes to enjoy a life of secluded luxury.

Born of artistic but yet-to-be-wealthy parents, he grew up in an insalubrious part of Queen's Park, west London. After leaving school he took a degree in law but decided real estate was a more interesting sphere of activity. He moved into property development, making his fortune from snapping up dilapidated houses and converting them into blocks of apartments.

In 2003 he had a go at buying The Telegraph broadsheet but was beaten to the prestigious newspaper by the even wealthier, even more reclusive Barclay brothers. The Barclays had agreed to buy out Lord Black's controlling stake, circumventing the auction launched by the Telegraph's immediate owner, Hollinger International.

Is this setback likely to deter Jeremy Lawson and prevent his company Aida Investments from rising and rising? The word in the City is, not a chance. Whether radical change is on the menu is yet to be seen, though experts predict he will take things steadily and continue to grow.

Although a natural conservative, he is highly unlikely to change his political allegiance or back the opposition to the UK's place in Europe, and he is a solid supporter of the European single currency.

Is he likely to go public? Very *un*likely, it's not in his nature. But were he to do so, be ready.

Was Jeremy thrilled by this review? He might well have been had he cared more about what people thought of him. He cared not and was not.

Chapter 13

Bubbles: The Subprime Debacle

"Life is like a soap bubble, blowing and maintaining as far as possible, but with the firm certainty that it will burst."

In the first decade of the new century, money flowed around the world in ever-spreading whirlpools. The world was awash with investment banks, hedge funds, financial advisors, prime mortgage brokers, collateralised loans. Jeremy looked at the firms that were faring best in the volatile markets and these were not the solid rocks of the past. They were not the banks and building societies, they were the hedge funds. The most successful hedge fund managers were shaking up the world. A new mindset was essential if Jeremy was to continue to thrive - he had to think like a hedge fund operator, tempered by reality rather than dreams.

The word coming from the USA showed that by 2005 the housing market had reached untenable levels of borrowing. The whole property scene in America had gone completely insane, where anyone who wanted a 100% mortgage could get one regardless of their earnings. You wanted to buy a house?

You went to your bank, and they gave you money for the house; they also gave you extra cash to do the renovations and refurbishment and furnishings. All you had to do was sign on the bottom line - no questions asked. If your dog wanted a mortgage for a luxury kennel, all it had to do was go into a bank and wag its tail, and why shouldn't dogs have their day?

Everything was based on historical data that property would not go down in value, or if it did it would not be dramatic. There was a veritable tsunami of cash. Money was everywhere. What was lacking was any semblance of a solid infrastructure. What was happening was the creation of a massively inflated property bubble, and the only certainty was that the bubble would inevitably burst.

Anticipating a housing collapse, Jeremy had to protect his investment portfolio by zigging as the market zagged. It was essential to be the 'alpha', to remain one step ahead of the howling pack. It was about having the guts to put his money on the table when others were trying to take theirs off and vice versa. Jeremy was displaying consummate skill in playing the game of buying when others were selling and selling what others were buying.

Believing that the market would crash, Jeremy covered himself with inexpensive insurance in case it did. Then, in 2008, it did indeed all come crashing down. Few foresaw the ferocity with which this would happen. It began with defaulting on loans, first in America, then one country followed another. The more you had borrowed, the more exposed you were and the harder you crashed. Certain phrases like these frequently appeared in the headlines throughout 2008: 'subprime mortgage crisis' – 'government bailout' – 'credit crisis' – 'bank collapse' - many others all pointing in the same direction: the collapse of capitalism as we know it. This period ranks among the most devastating in U.S. financial market history. Those who lived through these events will likely never forget the turmoil. Many chose not to and self-destructed.

Britain was far from immune to this devastation. Was Jeremy badly affected? Affected, without doubt. Badly, not. He was more sensitive than most to the overheating market, had borrowed less and had hedged his bets accordingly. So, when the property market boiled over and others were scalded, he got blisters. The insurance that he had purchased covered most of what he lost in the fall in the value of his properties.

In any case, to a large extent, he had transferred his property assets into art. For a man with what one would describe as traditional and conservative taste, it seemed rather surprising that he had an outstanding eye for rising painters and sculptors, and then you remembered that his parents were artists. Dealing in art was in his genes. While running his one-man hedge fund operation, the pieces he had bought for his pleasure became highly desirable lots at art auctions and he amassed yet another income stream as these came to the fore.

Chapter 14
Happiness?

"It is a clear gain to sacrifice pleasure in order to avoid pain."—Arthur Schopenhauer

Over the next fifteen years, Jeremy had no need to work terribly hard because his investments were working for him. He could afford to shop lavishly at Harrods. Savile Row, best known for being the undeniable home of hand-crafted British bespoke tailoring, was the go-to hub for any wealthy man serious about formal dressing, and Jeremy was serious. He could afford the privilege of having his shirts or a bespoke suit crafted by a Savile Row tailor of his choosing at any time he wished.

He did not hesitate to be flown to Copenhagen in his private Lear jet for a sumptuous meal at Noma where he would be welcomed in person by its chef Rene Redzepi. He would not think twice about spending fifteen hundred pounds at Petrus, Gordon Ramsey's Michelin-starred restaurant in Belgravia, for a lunch washed down by a bottle of Premier Grand Cru claret, usually enjoyed on his own. Despite his appetite for good food and wine, he never consumed to excess, had a personal fitness trainer in three times a week, maintained regular medical and dental checks in Harley Street, and had never had a day's illness.

Ever since that glorious performance of Aida, Jeremy had been passionate about opera, especially those of Giuseppe Verdi, and a visit to the Metropolitan in New York to hear Anna Netrebko or Roberto Alagna would always be coupled with purchases of one or two artworks by emerging artists from the private galleries of Christopher Henry or Sperone Westwater. The pieces would adorn his spacious apartment in Mayfair until eventually they were sent to auction at Sotheby's to further bolster his coffers. It wasn't that he needed the money, he needed the space.

The amazing thing for Jeremy was that no matter how much he spent, his bank balance only increased. He was not burdened by having relatives in need of support or with whom he had need of contact, and no children who would one day fight over his will. He gave generously to charities. He was a patron of several venerated institutions such as the Royal Opera House and the Tate Modern, and he had bequeathed sizeable amounts and all his art (especially the works of his parents) to the Tate so that others might one day on his demise share in his pleasure. He did however hope that such an event would not be for some time.

Most people are about as happy as they make up their minds to be. Was Jeremy a happy man? He was neither happy nor unhappy simply because he thought that happiness was not a concept worth striving for. Happiness oftentimes feels fleeting. His moments of bliss were just that, moments. Jeremy had simply decided not to be unhappy. Unhappiness, he knew from previous experience, was lasting and to be avoided, and he avoided it with great care. As he avoided friendship, Daniel excepted. As he avoided illness. All his life he had kept himself extremely fit and untroubled, and he had no intention of disturbing either his mental health or his physical equilibrium with ill-considered adventures into a way of life that other men followed without thought.

All things considered, Jeremy Lawson was content with his lot in life, and there were not unfounded rumours that he was at some point to be honoured by Her Majesty for his charitable services.

Then Chloe entered the scene.

Chapter 15
Chloe Jenkins

Clapham Junction, south London, was a mere five miles from Mayfair in distance, but a very different world indeed. It was one of those areas where the nouveau riche working in the City of London who couldn't afford Chelsea across the river lived in close proximity to less monied lower-middle-class families; where a market stall might be located next door a fine-dining French restaurant, where luxuriously refurbished homes resided next to council estates. The area had nothing of the gentility or class of Mayfair and consequently was a far more vibrant and edgy neighbourhood. Clapham Junction was within walking distance of neighbouring Brixton, notorious for its race riots in the nineteen-eighties, and shared more of Brixton's character than it did of Mayfair's. It had a vitality not measured in £s.

Clapham Junction station was the busiest in Europe measured by the number of trains using it, the busiest UK station for interchanges between services, and the only railway station in Great Britain with more interchanges than train entries or exits, and connected easily with the City.

The Peabody Estate on St John's Hill was within throwing distance of the big and bustling station, and it was where the parents of Chloe Jenkins lived in their unprepossessing two-bedroom flat. She had a sister, Jennifer - two years older - whom Chloe idolised. Jenny and Chloe were bubbly, sunny little characters, always giggling, adored by their mother and her friends. From the time they started attending school, their teachers were more than prepared to forgive their inherent naughtiness and lack of attention in class because from their earliest days the girls were capable of charming their way out of the trickiest of situations.

The two girls were the joy of their mother's life but not of their father's. Chloe was four years old when Tony the electrician disconnected the relationship, cut the money supply and lit out. One wondered what was in his mind, because not everyone had a loving, beautiful wife and two gorgeous little children, but since he was rarely there anyway during those years, he was not missed. Maintaining his family was not something that Tony ever took seriously, preferring rather to support bookies, trainers and racehorse-owners. Even before his departure, Chloe's mother Jane was forced into full-time employment as a saleswoman in the local department store to ensure the girls were properly cared for. The relationship between Jane and the girls was close, warm and caring, so it was not long before Tony became irrelevant; but even had he been needed, neither he nor his money was seen ever again.

Because Jane was at work all day, it was the dark-haired Jenny who ensured that her younger sibling became well educated streetwise. They mixed easily with the other kids on the estate and at school. Both girls were to enjoy sexual activity from an early age, but both were sensible and could in no way be described as promiscuous. Their experiences were shared openly with their mother who by this time was enjoying a friendship of her own with a married director of the department store.

Not that she was stupid or slow, but Chloe, like her peers, did not set much store in education, and left school at fifteen to attend a commercial college. There she acquired typing, book-keeping and computing skills, and had her first fling with a married man, the proprietor of the college. This lasted only as long as the course lasted, but she enjoyed the finesse of the older man by comparison with the frantic and inexpert gropings of her earlier liaisons.

A notable film of the late 1960s was a kitchen-sink drama called *Up the Junction,* after Nell Dunn's poignant book. It was the story of a young woman who traded her upper-class existence for a new life in Clapham Junction, that economically depressed suburb of London, in an attempt to distance herself from her moneyed upbringing and fight for her own living.

Chloe was about to attempt exactly the opposite.

Her first job was as an assistant receptionist in a small West-End hotel. Personable and surprisingly well spoken with little trace of a south London accent, she had a winning smile.

Chloe proved popular with the other hotel employees and seemed to be able to get on as well with the directors as with the cleaning staff. She was extremely competent in her job, and this attribute was done no harm by the fact that she had developed into a very pretty young woman with a shapely buxom figure. Her aquiline features under the shoulder-length blond hair were blessed by crystal blue eyes. She was tailor-made for being wishfully and lustfully desired by the guests, male and female alike. She was never short of invitations to dinner by men many years her senior, but except for an occasional dalliance, she had better ways of spending her evenings - as in enjoying the hotel penthouse suite and room service when it was occupied only by the hotel's financial director.

However, after a couple of years, the financial director was fired for having too much of an appetite for money that was not his, and he found it advantageous to emigrate to a city far away and learn Spanish in a country across the sea. Chloe realised then that her prospects for upward mobility, certainly in the short term, were limited. She was wrong. They were not limited, they were non-existent. The hotel group CEO had to show that such lascivious conduct was not to be tolerated, and her P45 was quickly delivered. She was given a reference that praised her skills but did not mention her voracious appetite for men of position.

Now what to do? She got chatting to one of her friends, Melissa, who worked as a receptionist in a swish dental practice in the West End.

"I started as a dental nurse," said Melissa, "but within a year I'd been promoted to receptionist. The patients make me feel special and often bring me presents. I love my boss, and just between you and me, he loves me too. Just saying ...."

Chloe thought about this and decided she too fancied the idea of becoming a dental nurse. It might not have been as glamorous as her previous job, but at least she would be a bigger spoke in a smaller wheel and have decent scope for personal growth. She answered an ad for a job in a chic practice in Soho, conducted herself with charm and great presence at interview and was offered the position.

Chloe's on-the-job dental training went smoothly. The informality of her new job appealed to her, her new boss was generous with praise and bonuses, and she loved strolling down Carnaby Street during her lunch hour. She was much liked by the patients because of her ability to make them feel at ease in that most challenging of environments. However, sterilising instruments and clearing dental work surfaces could only ever be of limited interest, and she jumped at the opportunity of becoming the practice receptionist when the offer came her way. This afforded her the opportunity of borrowing a few quid occasionally when patients paid in cash, and as long as she didn't overdo it, her employer and the other receptionist didn't seem to notice.

Many of her spare hours were spent together with her sister Jenny in the health club near their apartment, and both kept themselves well-honed and trim. It was there that she met and developed a relationship with an aspiring young actor named Danny. Danny was intelligent, fun to be with, and very good-looking, matching Chloe in all respects. The only problem was that Danny spent more time unemployed than working, as is the way with young actors, and it was Chloe who more often than not paid for their evenings out. Eventually, Chloe became bored with supporting Danny, and their relationship petered out.

At this time her mum Jane became ill and had to give up work, so it fell to Jenny and Chloe to provide for their home on the Peabody Estate where they had always lived. Chloe realised that it was more remunerative to be working as a locum receptionist than in full-time employment, so she reluctantly gave up her job in Soho in order to freelance. It was during this period that she sussed that not all dental practices had robust financial control systems, and without conscience she used her computing and commercial skills to withdraw cash over and above that in her wage packet with never a suspicion being raised. In fact, she became more skilled in extraction than those who employed her. She was ably assisted in this endeavour by her new boyfriend, Chris, who worked as a computer programmer for a city firm and expanded her repertoire of devious tricks. Although she appreciated his advice, his love-making skills were pedestrian and their relationship proved short-lived. Purpose served.

Within a year, Chloe had put together enough unearned income to pay for a holiday in Amalfi, Italy for herself, Jane and Jenny. Hard to believe, but this would be the first time any of them had ever left London, let alone the UK. Aside from the beauty and diversity of its coastline and gorgeous towns, the Amalfi Coast is known for its production of limoncello liqueur. The area is a copious cultivator of lemons, grown in terraced gardens along the azure Mediterranean. Limoncello unsurprisingly became their tipple of choice, and they spent many happy hours drifting from one store to another sampling the various brands. They took buses along the coast, and even splashed out to visit the famous Isle of Capri which they considered somewhat overrated. The little town that left them breathless, literally and figuratively, was Ravello, on a steep outcrop bedecked with stunning gardens. What a change from Clapham Junction and its rows of terraced houses!

When they arrived, they tended to stick mainly to Margarita pizzas. Chloe's taste was so basic that when the simple pizza that she had ordered arrived with fragrant basil leaves adorning it, she had flung these aside with the same disdain as one might have disposed of a sticky sweet wrapper. As the days went by, they became more adventurous in their culinary taste and on one occasion went as far as ordering *melanzane alla parmigiana*, but when they tasted the aubergine, only the cost of the dish prevented them from returning it to the kitchen. Yet, somehow, they all managed to consume it, and all agreed it was actually tastier than it looked. Progress in small steps...

They loved the simple breakfasts of croissants, focaccia, cheese and steaming Italian coffee, with the Mediterranean glistening before them. They could not get enough of the fresh figs that were literally falling from the trees. Ancient churches were not on their agenda, but they never tired of going from one fashion house to another. They spent hours in the early evenings inspecting the many little art galleries on the narrow, cobbled streets; most of all, they enjoyed the warm summer evenings drinking an obscene amount of cheap *rosante* as they revelled in the piazza restaurants.

Chloe, having tasted *la dolce vita,* wanted more, and promised her little family that this was the first but would not be their last trip abroad.

On her return to work, a letter awaited from the locum company that had provided her recent jobs. It read:

"Dear Ms Jenkins,

We have received a letter from Dr Richardson's practice in Bedford Square where you recently did a three-month locum. It appears that during the period you were on reception, their monthly deposits were 13% down on previous months and those months that followed. They have conducted a thorough audit but have not been able to pinpoint the shortfall, so no allegations of theft will be forthcoming, but they nevertheless felt it necessary to bring this to our attention.

The purpose of this letter is in no way accusatory, but we are proud of our outstanding reputation as the capital's chief dental locums provider and in turn feel it necessary to bring this matter to your attention and to inform you that we will no longer consider you for positions with our clients after your present one has terminated.

Sincerely

Annette Jones

CEO, Premier Locums."

She was given a week's notice of termination of her post at the practice. This would have been a huge setback for another less intrepid, but for Chloe, merely the need to find another position for herself.

Chapter 16
The King's Ransom

She responded to an ad in the Evening standard, attended an interview at The Starlite Dental Clinic on the King's Road, and moved down the road to swinging Chelsea. The surgery itself was extremely modern and trendy, a far cry from the one she had attended in Battersea as a child. The Starlite had recently been gutted, redesigned by a high-profile architect, and rebuilt. The equipment was state of the art. It was fully computerised, which suited Chloe's skills. Constantly changing modern paintings and sculptures from nearby Chelsea Art School adorned the walls of the reception area, offsetting the chic Danish furniture.

This looks like it's going to be a fun place to work, she thought, and so it proved. The clientele was generally young, super-trendy, many of them foreigners from the art school. It took little time before she became part of the set that frequented the numerous discos and clubs in the area with her older sister in tow.

The nearby clubs were generally opulent establishments famous for the large volume of personnel displaying extremely large mammary glands. This was mandatory for the staff.

Many of these glands had been significantly enhanced at great expense in Harley Street, and the bearers needed to earn enormous gratuities from appreciative patrons to recover the costs. The most appreciative of all were the professional footballers from Chelsea and Fulham who always had money to burn.

One such place was The King's Ransom Club - a name possibly given, as a local wag had suggested, because of what it cost to become a member. The Ransom was directly above the Starlite Dental Clinic, and many of the employees of The Ransom were patients at Starlite where they were given special rates for allowing the clinic's posters to be discretely displayed in The Ransom's cloakrooms.

One such employee was a hostess named Nadya, who had come from Mostar, Bosnia. Mostar had taken a fearful pounding when attacked by Bosnian Croats in the 1990s. Her father and two brothers had been killed, but her mother and Nadya had managed to make their way to England as refugees. Although within sight of middle age, Nadya was still in fantastic shape and very conscious of having a flashing smile that needed regular and careful maintenance. She took an immediate shine to the new receptionist whom she thought, given the right encouragement, could herself make a desired hostess. She invited Chloe to be her personal guest one Saturday night, and it was there that Chloe met Karl Janssens.

Chapter 17
Karl Janssens

In 1960, Petrus Janssens' parents had emigrated from Holland to South Africa when Petrus was ten years old. As a child, Petrus had been fascinated by the biblical stories told to him by his god-fearing Calvinist parents, and this was reinforced at Sunday school in Cape Town. After completing school, Petrus enrolled in a Dutch Reform Church Seminary to study theology. Three years later, at the age of 28, he was ordained as a lay preacher within the Calvinist Dutch Reform Church in a mixed-race community near Cape Town.

In the early eighties, physical relationships across the colour divide were still illegal in South Africa, and the close relationship Petrus developed with one of his parishioners had to be kept well under wraps. By the late eighties, however, the infamous Immorality Act had been rescinded, and Petrus and Marie were legally married in the very church where he preached, to the unbounded joy of the local community. Within a year, they had produced a son whom they named Karl.

Karl was growing up into a tall, sturdy and very handsome young man. He sailed through school, a private college run by the Dutch Reformed Church; He excelled at mathematics and science but showing little interest in matters theological. He disliked all his dedicated and earnest fellow scholars, preferring instead the street - in his location, a very interesting gang-run, drug-fuelled street. Karl's father still listened to Matt Monro, Karl was full-on Eminem. Theirs was less a generation gap, more a generation chasm. Polar opposites.

Sundays were for playing football (or soccer as the South Africans preferred to call the sport) and not for wearing a tie in church. His parents were disappointed, greatly disappointed, but what are children for if not to disappoint their parents? And by the same token, what are parents for if not to have any advice offered shunned? His parents wanted Jesus, Karl preferred Mammon. His father drove a second-hand Vauxhall, Karl wanted a real-deal, Robert De Niro-violent-gangster beast that roared when you trod on its foot and kicked you in the groin in a pleasurable kind of way.

Instead of choosing theological college, Karl applied for a business school bursary that was granted. He enrolled in a business studies and computer management programme at Cape Town University that he completed with distinction. He also distinguished himself as an extremely good footballer, was scouted early on and became a regular choice for Cape Town City in the national league.

As soon as he finished his course and been honoured with a Bachelor of Commerce degree *cum laude*, he said farewell to his parents (they were sad, he was elated) and set off for a trial with Crystal Palace Football Club.

He was given a three-month trial, during which time he made a few good friends but found few opportunities to make the grade. Achieving Premiership standards proved beyond his skills, so he was forced to settle instead for a regular place at Deptford Athletic, four divisions lower.

Karl, being little more than a journeyman footballer, found that the career he had chosen turned out to be less than highly remunerated. Although one believes that all footballers are ridiculously overpaid, this applies to the higher echelons only. Karl wanted the glitz of expensive restaurants, bars and casinos *(especially the casinos)* in Mayfair, Knightsbridge and Chelsea, not the shoddy markets and stalls of south-east London. Playing for Deptford Athletic was not going to give him the playboy lifestyle to which he aspired - to be an insider and not on the outside looking in. He wanted *Made in Chelsea,* not *Only Fools & Horses.* From what he had seen, London was an experiment in the co-existence of wealth and want, and what Karl wanted was wealth.

Would he have been better off taking up a job offer at a city hedge-fund firm? The firm was owned by a South African whom he had met and who, keen to give opportunities to his country-folk and especially those from more challenged communities, had offered him a worthwhile position. He declined the offer, feeling that being confined in an office all day seemed too much like work.

Then it got worse. His football activities came to a sudden end with a torn Achilles tendon. This wasn't great news for him, but it did give Karl time to think about applying one of his most abiding principles: if someone was dumb enough to allow others to access their wealth, whether willingly or unwittingly, they were fair game, and it behove him to be in the front of the queue to do precisely that. He considered this a duty. His father might have been religious about the God of Creation, but the temple at which Karl worshipped prayed to the god of avarice.

While recuperating, he spent his time using his computer technology skills first to invite funds into bogus charities that were very close to the real thing: providing a home for damaged creatures, especially cats; funds for underpaid nurses and brain-damaged children always brought in a thousand or two. Then he twigged that rather than trying get a lot of people to donate a little, better to go for a smaller market with a bigger pay-off each time. Less work, bigger rewards.

At that time, it was easy for the public at large to be seduced by the presence on glossy brochures of names of leading solicitors, accountants, corporate financiers and banks. The firms represented weren't necessarily bogus, but the presence of star names (preferably titled) on such brochures could easily have been. One lord of the realm who did exist but who was a complete fool was prepared to put his name and royal insignia onto any letterhead for anyone prepared to pay the price. He came close to being imprisoned for the privilege, bring pardoned only on the grounds of extreme stupidity.

This whole scene appealed to Karl. He began to sell holiday apartments in Spain online, posting glossy pictures of villas festooned in bougainvillea and clematis and surrounded by acres of palms and ferns and babbling brooks. The only snag for the purchaser was that these properties did not actually belong to Karl or anyone that he knew, and definitely not to Sir William Fitzsimmons. In fact, they didn't exist at all, but Karl was a wizard at creating computer-generated images. Posing as a developer, Karl managed to convince a sizeable number of applicants that unless they acted speedily, the opportunity to snag an unmissable bargain would quickly disappear into the annals of 'I wish I had acted quicker.' He was amazed at how gullible the public could be if the price seemed too good to be true. And if it so seemed, it usually was.

To prove that they were serious about a prospective purchase, punters would be invited to send in a four-figure deposit via a money transfer service. Most of the punters were people with hot money living abroad in far-flung countries who decided that it was not worth the cost of travelling to Spain to inspect the property that looked so good online. Unsurprisingly, that would be the last contact they would have with Karl and his crooked scheme. On a few occasions, they even handed over details of their identity documents that could be used (and were) to carry out more serious identity fraud. Such activity was well within the intrepid Karl's skill range.

He was surprised at how little time it took to amass a small fortune (well, small by Jeremy's standards, but for Karl, more than he had seen in his life) - in excess of two million quid. That turned out to be the easy part of the operation. What to do with it was more difficult. He was well aware that to splash out too lavishly would invite suspicion, so he transferred half of this hot money to an account in Spain.

Now, here's an interesting twist to this tale. Karl then decided that a variation on that Spanish theme would be to sell UK properties that he didn't own. One of those was a property in Hampshire owned by a Mr Sowerby. Boom. £750,000 in the bank. Add another £75,000 from someone named Jeremy Lawson. Boom boom. Way to go!! Then Karl got greedy. He had been smart in hiding the money trail, but except for the Spanish investment, not smart enough. When a significant number of cheated customers complained to a regulating authority, they somehow managed to pick up a connecting link leading to Karl. His little scheme was rumbled, and he ended up at the Old Bailey.

He was sentenced to four years in prison, which was reduced to twenty-four months when he agreed to return the £500,000 that the law enforcement officers had actually been able to trace (the other million and a half, being hot money, never having been reported as stolen.) He did briefly consider whether it was worth spending the extra twenty-four months in prison and retain the £500,000 but, tempting as it was, decided against the notion. The sentence might have been longer had any connection been made to Messrs Sowerby and Lawson, but the dots were never joined. Mr Lawson might never had heard of Karl Janssens, but Karl knew of Jeremy, and it would remain in his mind for future reference.

Karl served his time at Elmley, a bleak prison on the even bleaker Isle of Sheppey on the Kent coast. Because of his former footballing skills, he was allocated duties as a gym and football instructor, and actually enjoyed himself. Oozing charm and charisma, he got on really well with the other prisoners, but more important, with the officers. A good conduct report proved a mere formality, and as his release date approached, he began to think of the future. Because he was in possession of a Dutch passport, there was no risk of being deported back to South Africa. So, back to London? Amsterdam? Barcelona?

When he at last saw grey sky without the infringement of bars or wire-meshed walls, he returned to his small bedsit in Battersea. The only downside for Karl was that he dared not touch his Spanish investment, at least not for some time, for fear of it being traced by the authorities. Fortunately, he had sufficient cash squirrelled away to keep himself afloat for a year or two without doing what he dreaded most – sitting behind a desk in an office. This would give him time to think about his next manoeuvre which, ever the optimist, he knew would come.

During his early football days, Karl and his former Crystal Palace football mates had become accustomed to either celebrating the day's activities or seeking solace at an upmarket club in Chelsea called The King's Ransom. After he was released, he found them there as usual on a Saturday night, and normal service was resumed.

A few weeks later, Chloe Jenkins entered his life, and the current of lust that passed between them was instant and high-voltage electricity. The fact that Karl had a criminal record of which he spoke freely mattered not a jot to Chloe. There was instant chemical attraction, and it was not long before they were sharing their chemicals and being considered an item.

At the same time, Chloe's sister Jenny became twinned with another ex-Palace player, Luke, so it was all happy families. Jenny was by now working as a personal assistant to the MD of a firm of city architects based in Canary Wharf and earning substantially more than her younger sister. Although she was never jealous or envious of Jenny, Chloe came to the realisation that if she aspired to reach her sister's level of earning, it was necessary to upgrade workwise - being a deputy dental receptionist, or for that matter, a club hostess did not seem much of an improvement to her. Nevertheless, although now in her mid-twenties, she decided not to rush into making a change and knew that an opportunity would come if she remained patient.

That opportunity was to arrive gift-wrapped with the name of Mr Jeremy Lawson all over the package.

Chapter 18
Carmen

When Molly, the regular receptionist, went on extended maternity leave, Chloe was left in control. So competently did she perform that when Molly decided that motherhood was preferable to booking appointments, Chloe was offered a full-time job that she decided she would accept.

It was this very same dental practice that Jeremy Lawson attended every three months to have his teeth cleaned. Why had he left the Harley Street milieu to which he had always entrusted matters of health to venture down the less snobby and far trendier Kings Road for such a service? The King's Road practice actually wasn't that far, only a mere hop away, especially if one had a Bentley-driving chauffeur, and Starlite Dental had been highly recommended by a colleague impressed by the deft skills of the hygienist, Sandy.

Sandy whispered to Chloe to be especially nice to Mr Lawson, as he was wealthy and quite happy to reward good service with lavish gratuities for all. Other methods of wealth acquisition were necessary if Chloe's newly acquired taste for travel was to be maintained, and she wondered whether this could come about by becoming better acquainted with Mr Lawson. So, as soon as he had completed his hygiene appointment and been checked by Dr Lewes, she engaged him in conversation.

"I do like your after-shave, Mr Lawson, I bet it's Tom Ford.'

"That's a very good guess, young lady. It isn't Tom Ford, it's Italian, personally made for me in Milan, but I know one of Ford's that is very similar. How would you know it?"

"I bought a bottle for my ex-boyfriend's birthday - right waste of money that was!"

When she asked him how he planned to spend the rest of the day, he informed her that he was going to the Royal Opera House in Covent Garden that evening to see a performance of Carmen. "Do you like opera?" he asked.

"Don't know, never been. But always wanted to see one," she responded, a little disingenuously. Opera? Chloe?!

"Ah, we need to remedy that," said Jeremy. For the first time in his life, Jeremy felt something stirring just south of his belt buckle. Only the slightest of stirring though, not the full volcano. "Would you like to be my guest? Carmen is a great opera as an introduction to this beautiful art, and it happens I have a spare ticket." He didn't, but he thought he could dispense with the butler for the evening.

"Well, thank you, kind sir, but only if you promise not to tell Dr Lewes or Sandy, because it's strictly forbidden to go out with patients. I got a problem though - I don't have an evening dress."

"Oh, don't worry about that, no one dresses that smartly any more except for premieres, and I'm sure you'll look delightful in whatever you wear."

The warm smile she gave him would have caused immediate climate change. Icebergs would have melted. He became immediately aware that the stirring down south had increased. It was not an unpleasant feeling but it was unnerving, and Jeremy did not do unnerving. He made a firm decision that he would stick to his no-contact policy. It had served him well for the past fifty-four years, and he was of no mind to make changes.

After he left the surgery, he considered the possibility that he had acted in haste - appearing at the Royal Opera House with a woman less than half his age might appear somewhat louche, even debauched, to his staid acquaintances who would certainly be there as well. He thought about calling Chloe to tell her that something unexpected had come up (no pun intended) and that he was now unavailable; then he remembered how her face had lit up when he asked her to join him. Dammit, why not? It would be quite fun to set the opera set's tongues a-wagging! He chuckled quietly to himself.

Attired as was his custom in a bespoke Savile Row charcoal suit, pocket kerchief, crisp white silk shirt with gold cufflinks and grey jacquard tie – ever the epitome of sartorial elegance - Jeremy arrived at the Royal Opera House Covent Garden. His handcrafted oxblood lace-up shoes were so polished, you could see your face if you were silly enough to bend that low.

Coiffured wavy dark hair still full-bodied but these days streaked with grey; still unhandsome but improved with age. He looked fine and had taken great care to do so. This was familiar territory for hm. It was his natural environment.

By contrast, Chloe was standing nervously in the foyer when he arrived. This was foreign soil for her, the first time she had been in an environment where older women adorned in jewellery were dressed to the nines and striding about confidently. She had no need to feel disadvantaged. Jeremy noted that several men, mostly his age, were staring intently at her, and not without reason. She wore a simple but smart silk blouse and trouser suit she had borrowed from her mother (a gift from the department store director). Perfumed to the gills via the same route, blond hair washed and blown, she looked, in a word, stunning. When he saw her standing under the glittering chandeliers of the Royal Opera House, all doubts about the wisdom of the invitation were dispelled. He thought about Henry Higgins, with whom he had much in common. The opening scene of Pygmalion had taken place in front of this very building. He also thought about Richard Gere and Julia Roberts – although not his usual serious fare, he had enjoyed that film.

If one could choose a first opera to attend, Carmen would be very high on the list and probably in pole position. There was little reason to doubt why it is one of the most beloved of operas - arias like the Toreador Song and the Habanera known to all, flamenco dancing, a story of passion, rejection, rage and destiny - how could this heady brew fail to excite Chloe? And not just the music and the production - she had enjoyed the vintage Dom Perignon champagne, definitely an improvement on Prosecco and other cheap wannabes. She probably had a glass too many, and this might have caused her great embarrassment had she been inclined that way.

What happened was this: during one of the tenor's arias, he hit a gloriously powerful note - and then, as might have been written in the score, the music 'paused for dramatic effect'. Chloe could barely contain herself. "Ohmygawd", she half-shouted, fortunately only loud enough for those in the boxes on either side to hear. She was about to start clapping when she felt Jeremy's hand coming between hers. She closed her hands on his. The tenor continued, and Chloe emitted a very quiet giggle. This might have spelt the end of her brief operatic experience, but Jeremy, far from being offended, found the whole episode charming. Offence was neither intended nor taken. How innocent and naïve was this young woman!

During the intermission, he was impressed by the questions Chloe asked about the plot and its composer. When they went out to the sumptuously redesigned and glass-vaulted Floral Hall for smoked salmon sandwiches and a glass of chilled Batard Montrachet, he could see the enjoyment radiating from her every pore.

"This is such a treat! I thought opera was for the hoity-toities but I'm loving it", she beamed, adding, "I'm sorry if I embarrassed you Mr Lawson. I got a bit excited, didn't I."

"Jeremy, if you please" he responded, "and no, you didn't embarrass me in the slightest. In fact, it was rather nice to hear someone express their appreciation. I wish more of the stuffed shirts would, but in opera it's only at the end of an aria that you applaud."

"Bit of a bumpkin, ain'I? I promise to wait till you start clapping. Thanks for not being angry with me, Jeremy. You're so ... so... so polite."

The smile that crossed his face would have warmed the morning sun.

Then back to his private box for the final act. As the opera reached its climax, she involuntarily placed her hand on Jeremy's, and he had no desire to remove it. He heard her half-suppressed choke as the pathetic Don Jose plunged his knife into Carmen's guts and she fell lifeless at his feet. By the light reflected from the dim chandelier Jeremy saw the tears in her eyes that never made it further. He knew he had made an unlikely convert, and it warmed his icy heart. His gut feeling had been vindicated.

Nevertheless, she declined his invitation to join him for dinner, reminding him she had to work the following day. They shook hands and left, he to his chauffeur and Bentley, she to her bus. Chloe was quite prepared to play the long game.

The following day, having obtained his address from his dental records, she wrote a very gracious note on a specially purchased card thanking him for an evening she would never forget. She expressed the hope they could meet again sometime soon, even if just for a coffee.

A couple of weeks later, Jeremy was rather surprised to find a handwritten note in his mail and was pleased when it turned out to be from Chloe.

Dear Mr Lawson

I am so enjoying life on the King's Road, and the surgery has some very 'interesting' patients. I can't tell you why they're 'interesting' (my boss wouldn't like that!), but they're quite arty. But it has some very smart patients as well, and I must say that you are top of that list.

I often think of that wonderful evening at Covent Garden and I am now the proud possessor of 'Carmen – The Highlights', which I can now sing practically off by heart, but that's not anything you want to hear!

You were so kind to me that night, and made me feel like a princess, or at least a duchess (although to tell the truth I wouldn't have the faintest idea what either feels like!)

Anyway, enough of this idle chit-chat, I know how busy you are. But if you ever fancy a coffee and croissant (my treat!) down on King's Road SW3, my phone number is 07700 610 942 (text chloe25@gmail.com).

I hope you will call sometime!!
With very warmest regards,
Chloe.

Immediate stirrings, but not stirrings that were out of his control. He did not phone her, nor did he accept her invitation, but what he did do was send a text inviting her to join him for a performance at the ROH of *La Traviata* when he returned from Italy.

Another gorgeous outfit, this time borrowed from a friend. Another wonderful performance - tears actually streamed from her eyes when Violetta snuffed it. If anything, Chloe said, she enjoyed it even more than Carmen, and when he produced a CD of the opera for her, signed by Joan Sutherland and Luciano Pavarotti, she gave his hand a squeeze and lightly kissed his cheek. But when he invited her for dinner, she once again demurred because it would interfere with her work the next day.

As they walked to the door, Jeremy smiled. "I've got an idea, young lady – in a month's time, your opera will be *La Boheme.* That's another gorgeous tearjerker. It will be on a Saturday night but unfortunately it will be at the Metropolitan in New York. Do you think you could force yourself to join me?"

"You're joking me, Mr Lawson, I mean Jeremy!"

"I never joke. We'll fly there in my jet on Saturday morning, attend the opera in the evening. I have a spare bedroom in my apartment on 44th Street and I promise to leave you completely unmolested, just in case you think my intention is to seduce you. I don't do that sort of stuff, never have, waste of physical and emotional energy. On Sunday we fly back. No work missed! Good?"

"Good? GOOD??!! Fucking – oops, sorry! – *totally* unbelievable! But this will cost you an absolute fortune! Why are you so kind to me?"

"Seeing your face as you watch the opera is worth every penny."

This time, the kiss was on his lips, and he liked it. She could practically hear the cash registers ringing.

Chapter 19
The French Deal

The month leading up to the New York jaunt were busy times for both Jeremy and Chloe, but not with each other. Jeremy was involved in negotiating the purchase of a block of some seventy apartments in south Kilburn, a somewhat forgotten area in northwest London. Forgotten, that is, except by its disproportionately large Muslim population who had over the years built a number of schools, some encompassing the traditional national curriculum as well as selected Islamic subjects. Numerous small places of worship were scattered throughout the suburb. Two things interested Jeremy. First, its proximity to Paddington Hospital – doctors, nurses and ancillary professionals, many of them Muslim, who usually made excellent tenants. Good for the short term.

The second was that South Kilburn was situated in the triangle between Notting Hill Gate, Queen's Park and Maida Vale, areas that had soared in value over the years and where new purchases were virtually unaffordable except to the wealthy. South Kilburn was therefore most likely next to become gentrified in the near future, so the long term would take care of itself.

The negotiations had begun smoothly enough with the French company that owned the block. With Brexit happening, they wanted out. Difficulties had arisen over the question of existing dilapidations. Each party wanted the other to foot the bill. Jeremy's surveyors had of course noted each and every defect, and the French had in turn downplayed each. An overly fastidious French lawyer wasn't helping either, delaying completion interminably. Jeremy was on the verge of calling off negotiations, until the French carelessly showed their hand, and it wasn't a strong one.

The matter had allegedly been complicated with the apparent arrival of a potential other purchaser, they said, but Jeremy knew a bluff when he saw one – he'd experienced this often in the past. He was adept at finessing a trick in bridge, but this French move had no finesse and seemed crass. He saw the mere fact that the French were prepared to introduce such a ploy as a sign of weakness, and that he would have them on toast if he was prepared to hold out for substantial reductions. Hold out he had, and the signs were that the French were about to cave. He would be flying with his lawyer and surveyor to Lille, confident that he was about to conclude a very worthwhile deal. In the event, his confidence was not unfounded, and by the end of the week he had added the apartment block to his portfolio of properties.

Celebration was in order with the solicitor and the surveyor and took place on the Friday evening at Lille's *La Table* where their young but brilliant chef Thibaut Gamba had established a formidable reputation with his creative culinary skills, especially with fish dishes. The dinner proved to be superb, and when Jeremy saw a South African white wine called *Buitenverwachting* which from previous tastings he knew to mean 'beyond expectation', he thought this very fitting for the way negotiations had gone. This paled into insignificance when he ordered a bottle of '67 Chateau d'Yquem at a mere 4,000 Euros, of which the solicitor and surveyor had heard but never experienced. And an experience it was! Intense, unctuous, fruity, a perfect dessert in its own right. Yet, even as he celebrated, Jeremy thought how much Chloe would have enjoyed the experience.

Chloe almost certainly would have enjoyed the experience were she not enjoying an experience of her own. She, Karl, Jenny and Luke were that same evening drinking Prosecco, smoking joints, sniffing coke and participating in a no-holds-barred uninhibited foursome in their suite at the Old Bell Inn in Malmsbury. The evening had been paid for by a horse named Glorious Return that had managed to keep its nose in front of Creative Talent's in the 3:30 at Newmarket. Karl and Luke had each bet £500 at 20-1 based entirely on a hunch that Glorious Return would provide just that, and - *go, you beauty!* - it did. Did either of them have that kind of money to play with? Not really, but nor did most people who bet on horses or dogs or football. And now that they had had this big win, were they going to put it away for a rainy day? Not a snowball's chance in hell! Life was to be enjoyed (a sentiment shared by Jeremy) and enjoying it they all were.

Chloe too was thinking of Jeremy, but not of how much he might have enjoyed her foursome experience. No, her thoughts were more on the lines of how he could be influenced to ensure that a sizeable chunk of his fortune was directed her way. She wasn't a great one on proverbs, but two that she remembered were 'there's no fool like an old fool' and 'a fool and his money are soon parted', and she thought that both were pretty fine mantras. The only flies in the ointment were that Jeremy was not that old, and, as she well knew, was certainly no fool. She would have to think smart if progress was to be made.

Karl was none too amused when he heard that Chloe was jetting off to New York, but when she assured him that Jeremy was anything but a dirty old man, and that her mission was strictly business and not pleasure, he relaxed. If she was making an investment in their future, that was fine as far as he was concerned. After all, he had skin in the game.

She didn't express her thought that she was expecting a great deal of pleasure from being at the opera - he couldn't possibly have understood that such an experience could actually produce joy.

Bring on New York!

Chapter 20
The Big Apple

The idea of flying in a private jet was also something to be savoured, and in the event did not disappoint. It was a million cuts above her only previous flight experience. Her trip to Italy had been EasyJet economy. This time, butler Marco was on hand with drinks and canapes, and if the notion of smoked salmon and caviar had never had the opportunity to excite her in the past it certainly would in future, especially if washed down by Armand de Brignac champagne.

She was surprised at how easily they chatted, but what really made her feel optimistic was that he seemed very interested in her past. She opened to him as she had not to too many others. She told him how much she had enjoyed her recent trip to Italy, neglecting to inform how it had been funded. He smiled when she said she felt it would be a while before she travelled again. Two things that did not get mentioned were her penchant for other people's money, and Karl. Jeremy did not seem put off by her humble origins, indeed quite the opposite, asking many questions. He, of course, was worldly beyond belief and could tell endless stories of the VIPs he had met and dined with, respected businessmen who were lecherous rogues, and perfectly straight actors who were gay as could be.

She asked him why he felt it necessary to have mentioned that he had no intention to seduce her - it had never entered her mind that he would, she said, and in any case, she was sure he could get any woman he wanted.

His response rather astonished her.

"To tell the truth, Chloe, I have never ever wanted to 'get' a woman. Sex has never been of interest to me, not ever."

He explained about his rejection at age six, and how the bulldog remark by a little girl had shaped his future. As he finished his little story, the thought flashed through his mind that this was the only time he had ever mentioned the event to anyone aside from his mother, and to a young woman less than half his age that he barely knew. What he did know was that he had never felt so at ease with anyone before, someone he knew he could trust implicitly. There's no fool ...

Because of the zone differential, they arrived at lunchtime and there was still opportunity to see something of New York. Jeremy said he wanted to save Times Square for the later evening, so the pre-ordered limousine was ready and waiting to take them downtown. Although early spring, the weather was fine. The flowers were blossoming, and walking the High-Line was delightful, with views of the uptown skyscrapers even more vivid than her movie recollections. They walked across to Chelsea Market to enjoy what almost defines New

York, a Reubens on rye with sliced pickle. So many calories, for sure, but sooo delicious ...

A big yellow taxi ferried them back to his apartment, where there was just time for Chloe to luxuriate in a hot bubble bath. She coyly asked whether he would consider washing her back but said it in a way that made him realise she was just teasing. He of course never considered venturing beyond the solid oak bathroom door once it closed. Nevertheless, signs of activity south of the border ... Was it possible he was feeling a tiny bit randy? No, the Shelley-conditioned leopard was definitely not about to change spots.

As soon as she dressed in a simple but alluring frock she had borrowed from a friend, they relaxed over a glass of chilled Cloudy Bay white wine, which Jeremy had first sampled while on a trip to New Zealand. Jeremy provided a precis of *La Boheme,* the love story of the poverty-stricken poet Rodolfo and the consumptive Mimi set in a Paris garret. What he could not prepare her for was the beauty of Puccini's score, and as he had predicted she had not managed to hold back her tears when Rodolfo took hold of Mimi's 'frozen' hand, and actually sobbed when the poor girl succumbed in his arms to her unforgiving illness. She had heard that in operas, every-one dies in the end, but how tragic was this?!

As they walked out, they paused in front of the two huge Marc Chagall paintings in the foyer, and as he iterated to her the story of the life of the Russian-Jewish artist and the pogroms his works depicted, she emoted once more. How innocent this girl is, how thirsty for knowledge ...

A dinner at Gabriel Kreuther's two-star Michelin restaurant, august, modernist where even the saltcellar was a gilded 'big apple'. The maitre and Jeremy were obviously on familiar terms. He showed the unlikely couple to the plush leather banquette that he said was Jeremy's always. A few tables away sat a woman whose face bore unmistakeable signs of regular reconstruction by addition and subtraction. Fortunately, neither of them heard her bitchy remark to her companion: "It's amazing how attractive an ugly little man can become when standing on his pile of money."

Her handsome younger companion was about to respond, "I think I hear the pot calling the kettle black," but decided it was not in his interest to do so.

Chloe was acutely conscious that others were staring at her but cared not a jot - she was queen for the night. The perfectly prepared food was unfussily delivered, with culinary surprises for the young woman: langoustine tartare with cauliflower creme, followed by foie gras, delivered in unctuous chestnut and quince sauce. Chloe who only a short while ago was tossing aside basil leaves! Hmm, she could definitely get used to this, and it beat the hell out of a takeaway pizza in Karl's flat.

The view of Times Square from the taxi window was as intoxicating as he had led her to expect. She held tightly on to his hand all the way back to his apartment, and he did not object, but he did not even consider following her into the spare bedroom. For a moment she considered going into his but decided that it was not a good idea. In fact, on the balance of probabilities it would have proved disastrous.

There was just time the following morning for scrambled eggs on sourdough at the Bar & Grill before boarding the Lear.

They spoke for a while on the return journey. Whether it was the on-going euphoric feeling of the delightful weekend or perhaps the excellent champagne they were imbibing, their conversation began to get a little more personal.

A random thought came into his mind, something that had even preceded the Shelley incident. He told Chloe about his early childhood. He had this imaginary friend, Tardis. With no siblings for playmates, Tardis was his constant companion.

"Why was he named Tardis?"

"Well, I'd heard the name when I went with my father to watch Dr Who on a friend's tv. We didn't own one, my mother was quirky that way. My Tardis didn't in any way look like Dr Who's telephone booth, he resembled a beanstalk: very tall and very thin but oh so strong."

When he turned five, his parents decided it was time for a dog, and the name Tardis was transferred to the black and tan sheepdog pup his dad brought home from a sheep farm. Tardis mark 2 could sit for an entire day panting and waiting for a ball to be thrown, the further the better. Jeremy had to fling a lot of tennis balls, something he utterly loathed doing but did not have much choice if he was going to keep Tardis happy. Then the dog had got itself run over and had never been replaced. Attachments only caused pain .... Another lesson in life.

Chloe put her hand on his. "Wow, that must have been painful for a little boy. I would not have thought that you could ever have been lonely – you seem to relate so easily to people. I suppose it's because you're so intelligent. You know, Jeremy, I never thought about this before I met you, but I'm beginning to regret that I didn't give more time to getting educated. I'm really envious that you know about so many things."

"There's still time, Chloe. Lots of people do really well as mature students, you know."

"What, like study? No way, Jose!"

"You might regret that one day."

"Have you ever done anything that *you* regretted?" asked Chloe.

"Oh, for sure! I haven't always been Mr Nice Guy", Jeremy chuckled.

"I find that hard to believe, Jeremy - you're always so generous and kind."

Flattery has the nasty habit of loosening tongues, especially when accompanied by a vintage Dom Perignon. Jeremy, who was always taciturn, never saying more than was absolutely necessary, dropped his guard. Despite a lifetime of cautious circumspection in conversation, his tongue began to take on a life of its own. he recounted a story of a deal he had done.

"Well, when I first went into the property business, there was a sitting tenant in the building I wanted to buy and renovate in Battersea. She was an old dearie, but so obstinate! I offered her a beautiful apartment in a nearby block I owned, far nicer than hers, but she'd been there for sixty years and wasn't budging."

"Silly old cow! What did you do?"

"Sent around a friend who had very big shoulders to discuss the matter. I won't go into the details of the discussion, but my friend could be very persuasive. The good news for her was that his strong muscles were put to good use to move her furniture."

"Ooh, naughty, Jeremy ..."

The loose tongue was now wobbling dangerously out of control. At this point, Jeremy should have remembered that a wise mouth gathers no feet. But he didn't. His lips widened, and his next mis-step was to place his foot firmly into his oral cavity. Jeremy told Chloe the story of his dealings with Daniel Odenfemji and the activities of Daniel's father.

Mistake. Huge.

Chloe said nothing but stored the information in that special place in her brain where she cached ammunition.

After another glass of wine, she fell asleep nestled on his shoulder ... but before she nodded off, the thought entered her head that she was entirely re-living the story of the gorgeous hooker Vivian Ward in *Pretty Woman* - hadn't she also been flown to an opera? - the only difference being that she knew Vivian's intentions were far less devious than her own. Vivian's story had ended happily, but Jeremy the bulldog wasn't Richard Gere. Much as she was getting to like Jeremy, she was determined the ending for him would not be one straight out of Hollywood, and the story of Daniel Odenfemji might provide the key to unpicking his lock.

Chapter 21
Music to Karl's Ears

The following night at The King's Ransom, she related the story to Karl. He said nothing but, unobserved, wrote the name of the Nigerian on the back of his cigarette pack.

When she got into work the next morning, Chloe was still feeling the effects of overindulgence. She was somewhat snappy with the dental technician who was a few minutes late in delivering a set of porcelain crowns destined for the front teeth of a middle-aged woman who wanted to be ten years younger and was complaining of being kept waiting. The technician, who had been with the dental practice for years, was not having this, and reminded her sharply that it was she who served him, not the other way round, and that he would still be working for the dental surgeon and would continue to do so for many years after she returned to working in Clapham Junction where she belonged.

Suitably chastened, Chloe realised that she was not yet in a position where she could afford to lose her job, and calmed. She thought about this woman and her new crowns: how nice to be able to afford to spend £20,000 on self-improvement –

and god knows this woman needed it, for all her expensive apparel. Chloe was grateful that if she ever had (and hoped that sometime soon she would have) £20,000 to improve herself, it would not be on her teeth, because they were already a great advertisement for the practice, but spent acquiring a tan and vitamin D on a holiday to Monterey in California where she could be pampered in style in the luxury spa she had just been reading about in Vogue. One might think that she could have asked her new best friend for a loan, knowing he would never ask for the money to be returned, but Chloe was playing for far bigger stakes.

The unlikely friendship continued over the next few months. Included in Chloe's education were visits to Glyndebourne for picnic lunches in the glorious garden followed by carefully selected operas by Mozart and Rossini. Jeremy, however, didn't do just opera. A weekend in Scarborough for a play by Alan Ayckbourn, and another in a smart little hotel in Stratford-upon-Avon and a performance of *Macbeth* at the Swan Theatre were added to her *'I've seen ...'* list; and she was loving it. Particularly and peculiarly, Chloe identified with Lady Macbeth, although she was rather bemused by her much-quoted line, *"Come you spirits, that tend on mortal thoughts, unsex me here."* When Jeremy explained to her that what she was saying when crying out *"unsex me here"* was that she was spurning her feminine characteristics and wishing that the milk in her breasts would be exchanged for gall so that she could murder Duncan herself, and that Lady Macbeth believed that manhood is defined by murder.

A bit extreme, she thought. Borrowing a few quid or even lots of pounds without permission was one thing, but murder?

What did Karl have to say about all of this? Well, besides accusing her of becoming a bit nose in the air, he accepted her story that it was all part of her gaining her sugar-daddy's trust, and that she would be ready to make her move in the not-too-distant future.

Chapter 22

A Doctor and A Lawyer...

It was time for Jeremy's annual check-up with his doctor in Harley Street. He had been seeing Dr Victor Smythe every year without fail since he was twenty-five and had developed a great liking for this urbane gentleman who was of the old school. A graduate of Imperial College, now a consultant at his alma mater and at the King Edward the Seventh Hospital, Victor was assiduous in maintaining his knowledge and attended courses regularly all over the new world. He was never shy to add that, besides keeping him relevant professionally, these forays and courses in foreign climes had the beneficial effect of mitigating his tax liability.

These days, a townhouse in Knightsbridge, a country estate in the New Forest, a titled wife and two sons at Cambridge (although neither studying medicine) - Victor's cup was overflowing. Always dressed immaculately in a suit, starched white shirt with cufflinks to match his pin-striped tie, he was fluent in French, Italian and German, and like Jeremy, had a great love of opera. Many of his patients were of that milieu, and if ever a diva was unable to sing of an evening 'due to ill-health' or was 'indisposed', chances were it was Dr Victor Smythe who had signed the certificate.

The two men would regularly chat about the performances they had seen during the previous twelve months, and Jeremy never protested at the stonking large bill he received by post a week later. Very occasionally, one of Dr Smythe's patients failed to pay timeously, and although Victor's secretary never sent a second account, that patient would never be seen again.

After a brief chat about a mutual acquaintance whose third wife was younger than his youngest son, Dr Smythe was ready to conduct his usual thorough examination. Apologising, he donned rubber gloves and smeared his right finger with Vaseline before gently inserting it where the sun never shone. On this occasion however it was not a brief foray into Jeremy's anal sphincter. When the finger was removed, the gloves disposed of, and the hands washed, he turned to address his patient.

Jeremy was quietly dressing. He noticed a tiny flaw in his silk underpants as he flipped the elastic around his waist. This upset him. The pair was part of a set of six that he had bought at great expense when in the Zona Montenapoleane in Milan a while ago and he hoped that the others weren't heading the same way. Did quality no longer mean what it used to?

Having a trusted friend stick his finger up his bum was such an undignified and demeaning experience, especially a person with whom he had just discussed the current performance of

The Marriage of Figaro they had both seen at Glyndebourne. Anyway, so be it - if needs, must. A man is at such a disadvantage in such circumstances, feels ridiculous. One is always tensed, fearing the terrible words, the sentence that will cut away one's future from under his feet. Or in this case above them.

At the doctor's mercy, he turned to face Dr Victor Smythe.

"Not such great news, old chap, there's a definite hardening of the left lobe of your prostate. Quite large I'm afraid. No need to panic, but I'm a bit concerned that it has developed quite so quickly since last year. I've also had a look at the results of your urine and blood tests and they unfortunately do show a few specks of blood in the pee and an elevated PSA."

"What's the reading?"

"It's 9.8 – that's very high. We get concerned when it rises over 5."

Jeremy blanched but remained calm; "Does a high PSA always equate to prostate cancer?"

Dr Smythe explained, "Getting one's PSA levels tested on a routine basis is what the medical system says is the best way to catch prostate cancer early and eradicate it with minimal intervention. The prostate-specific antigen test has long been considered as the gold standard for detecting prostate cancer. But is it really? The public has long been told that high PSA levels are suggestive of prostate cancer onset, but the current view is that is an extremely unreliable indicator, and even the doctor who designed the test has said as much."

"Are there other more reliable tests?"

"Men who fall into this category are often encouraged to get biopsied and undergo invasive treatment like surgery and radiation. This in itself is not without risk. The problem is that a biopsy, or the prostate trimming or removal operation itself, can actually *cause* a dormant cancer to spread to other Parts of the body. It must be said however that this is very unusual."

"So, without pussyfooting around, Victor, what do you advise? What do I need to be doing?"

"I think the best advice I can give at this moment is to do nothing. Let's test your blood and urine in three months and see you again for an MRI scan. In the meantime, enjoy Bryn Terfel in *Don Pasquale*, I believe he's marvellous." With that, he shook Jeremy's hand and unusually for him gave him a brief hug. That worried Jeremy more than anything Victor had said.

The visit to Victor got Jeremy thinking. Perhaps his belief that he would live to a venerable age might just be a little optimistic. This did not particularly upset him because, based on what he had observed of his many older acquaintances, becoming aged and infirm was not a highly desirable state. If this was the case, perhaps he should be thinking of what would become of his not inconsiderable estate once, as so eloquently stated by Hamlet, he shuffled off this mortal coil. As things stood, all his assets would be shared by more than a dozen different charities and trusts – he had no relatives, or at least none that he cared for, and all his acquaintances were wealthy in their own right. Except for one – Chloe.

Over the past year, Chloe had brought a joy to his life that he never believed possible – her *joie de vivre,* her vitality, her eagerness to share his enjoyment of opera, her appreciation of fine art had elevated his spirits on every occasion. She had never asked him for a single penny, and despite one or two comments that had come to his ears, she could not by any standard be considered a gold-digger. In fact, on more than one occasion she had refused to accept offers of gifts. She was dedicated to her work, that was obvious, but he could see no reason why she should have to work five days a week for the rest of her life. She had an innocence about her, he thought, that was refreshing, not to mention unusual, in this grabbing world. Why should she not share his wealth?

So, Jeremy decided that a visit to his solicitor was clearly necessary.

After arranging an appointment, Jeremy arrived at the elegant building at St Pauls' Churchyard in the City. He was not kept waiting and was shown into the large and tastefully furnished office of his solicitor. The view of St Paul's Cathedral through the floor-to-ceiling plate-glass window never ceased to cause him a momentary loss of breath, but how long would it be before the avaricious property developers blocked it with yet another high-rise building? After a warm handshake and exchange of pleasantries, he was invited to sit by the stern-looking, tall and balding man. He reclined, sinking into the well-padded upholstery of the leather chair as he outlined his thoughts to Sir Christopher Reed-Gibbs, the senior partner and founder of the legal firm Reed-Gibbs Braceworthy plc that had acted for him on more occasions than he could remember. Jeremy had learned to respect if not particularly to like Reed-Gibbs, for whereas the man had overdosed in legal cunning he was certainly deficient in warmth. Jeremy didn't need warmth.

When he told Sir Christopher of his intention to include Chloe Jenkins in his will, he was not surprised at the vastly experienced and chillingly cold solicitor's response: "I don't want to sound like John McEnroe, Jeremy, but you cannot be serious! Please don't tell me you've become a sugar daddy at this stage of your life! Have you finally surrendered your virginity?"

"No chance of that, Christopher, I'm still as pure as the driven snow. The thing is that, despite your extremely high fees - some have even said extortionate or at best exorbitant - I've got more money than I could spend in three lifetimes, and although I understand your misgivings, she has become the daughter I never had. I really want this to be life-changing for a young friend who has brought me a precious gift."

"And what might that be, my dear man?"

"Chloe has me feel years younger – she has a warm sense of humour that is totally infectious and makes me feel rejuvenated."

"That may well be so, but the courts are rife with cases of young women taking advantage of much older men by pandering to their vanities."

"All these years you have been my advisor in matters of chancery, Christopher, I have very rarely gone against your sage advice, but this time I will. My estate is worth close on four hundred million pounds, and I have divided it between eighteen charities, and as you are aware, also allowed for a generous and decent bequest to both you and Victor Smythe that will ensure neither of you end up in penury. Ha, perish the thought! What I propose is that from the balance due to the charities, a modest amount of 5% be set aside for young Chloe."

"But that's close on twenty million pounds, Jeremy!"

"Indeed, and I don't think the charities will be too upset. At least this beneficiary has a face, and a very lovely one at that."

Reed-Gibbs bit his tongue. "Complete the following: no fool like ... ."

"You may be right, but now kindly make the change as I have instructed you to do."

Twenty million quid to a bit of common skirt? We'll see about that, my dear man ...

Chapter 23
A Big Deal

After he left the oak-panelled offices of Reed-Gibbs Braceworthy plc, solicitors-at-law, Jeremy was deep in thought, and, it has to be said, deeply apprehensive. Being told that he had a cancer that was the no.1 killer of older men, one that could conceivably be written on his own death certificate in the not-too-distant future, this had a very concentrating effect on his mind. A man aged sixty who had never had a day's serious illness in his life was not exactly experienced in dealing with such a prognosis. How would this affect his future plans? Would he rein in? Would he no longer look for new opportunities to do deals, to amass more wealth? Or would he take the view, as Dr Smythe had suggested, adopt the 'wait and see' position, hope that the PSA reading was a false one, or at least not serious, and get on with his life and his business?

After careful consideration he decided on three things: first that he would fight on as normal and shed all thoughts of mortality from his mind; second, he would say nothing to anyone including Chloe about his illness; and third, he would not inform Chloe that she had become a beneficiary in his will.

As is the way of things, something then came up that was to put all thoughts of illness and indeed of Chloe from his mind. Two days later, he received an invitation from Daniel Odenfemji to meet for lunch at Daniel's apartment in Knightsbridge, a *pied-a-terre* frequently used for meetings or overnight stays. The fact that it was large and opulent enough to put it beyond the reach of all but the super-rich did not escape Jeremy's attention once again when he arrived. He was not the only person there. Already present was Sheikh Abdullah Bin-Ibrahim, who aside from being one of Dubai's wealthiest investors was also a highly educated scientist. The sheikh's interest in nano-technology and DNA research had been well documented in accredited scientific journals.

The delectable lunch of delicately stewed yam and plantain followed by seared bluefin tuna prepared by Daniel's Nigerian chef (who had accompanied him to London) was memorable. The accompanying bottle of Marquis de Laguiche that Jeremy had brought along and knew to cost not less than £2200 made his palate sing arias in a duet with his tongue. The sheikh was happy to have his proffered share of the wine redolent of linden and acacia (or so the bottle said). As they sipped their cognac they got down to the business in hand.

Sheikh Abdullah wished to purchase a bio-technology company in Manchester known for its brilliant research, especially in the field of RNA viruses such as SARS. This was especially pertinent now there was talk of a newer, potentially more lethal virus looming on the horizon. If vaccines could be developed against such lethal bugs, the potential rewards could barely be imagined. For the sheikh, there would be the additional pleasure of getting to such a vaccine before the Israelis, which would be a memorable first.

Under the strict new laws covering money laundering, the sheikh needed a British citizen to act as chairman of the board. If Jeremy was prepared to take on the role, Daniel said, he would be remunerated to the tune of a quarter million pounds - *per month*. Daniel assured him it was a totally legitimate operation, and also said that he, Daniel, had no personal involvement other than that of a broker, and as an advisor if so desired.

Even by Jeremy's high earning standards, this was significant, and if small beer by comparison with what footballers were earning, not to be sniffed at. His first thought was how much his charities (not to mention his newfound friend) would benefit. He then thought that he should inform Daniel and the sheikh of his potentially lethal illness, but the necessity for this fell away when the sheikh said Jeremy could walk away from the post at any time as long as a successor could be immediately identified. As he said to Jeremy, "This is a legitimate business opportunity; I am not in the business of money-laundering - I have no need to. I am a scientist whose concern above all else is to leave a legacy to mankind. But before you give me your response, I suggest you speak to your lawyers, your bankers and any other advisors you many have."

Daniel added, "I have known both of you for more than twenty years, done business with each of you, and can vouch for the integrity of you both. I also hope you can trust me to be an honest broker, but I say that if either of you betray my trust, it will not go well with you."

The thought of having to deal with a Nigerian minder with something serious on his mind was not one that Jeremy found enticing. "I have to ask this question, Daniel, so forgive me – is your father involved?"

"Not a chance, my brother. His way is not my way."

"Please don't take offence, but I'm pleased about that. I will investigate, I'd be a fool not to, but I think we have a deal."

The three men stood, shook hands and raised their glasses to each other. Each felt elated.

Having done due diligence very carefully as he was wont to do, Jeremy was duly installed as Chairman of the Board, and the takeover of Vaxxopharm Technologies was announced in the Financial Times and The Telegraph. Jeremy beamed as though he had just won the pools, although he didn't need to because all was good in his universe.

Chapter 24
Invitation For A Pizza

Hi Jeremy.

I hope you won't mind me texting you. It's been a while since I've seen you. Not that I am looking for anything, just checking to see you're ok. Also to make sure that I have not done anything to annoy or upset you. I'd hate to do that!

Be well. X Chloe

Hi Chloe

No, of course you haven't upset me! Things have been rather hectic business-wise, but I'm pleased to say I've done a very nice deal with a sheikh. The deal was set up by my Nigerian friend, Daniel. I have to visit him in Milan this weekend to sign some papers, so perhaps you'd like to join me? There's a nice little place on the corner where we can get a real Italian pizza.

Jeremy

Ha ha! As if you'd eat at a pizzeria or even a trattoria! (See, I know some Italian words). Of course I'd love to join you, but I have to warn you that since I've met you my taste in food has become just a little more sophisticated so I'd like to go for a spag bol at least. Must I wear anything special? xx

OK spag bol it will be! No need to wear anything special - your usual good taste will suffice. Just be careful you don't spill any of the spag and especially the bol. You may even manage to do some shopping - I'm sure you know that Italy is the home of a few well-known fashion-houses, I'm thinking Versace and Armani and Gucci, not to mention Dolce & Gabbani, Prada and Valentino, but did you know their headquarters are all in Milan?

Please be at my apartment at 8am on Saturday, and we will return late on Sunday evening. xx

You are so funny, Jeremy! All those names are way out of my league - I'm strictly a Zara girl. Anyway, it'll be fun to look. Can't wait! xxx

Well, we might even do something exciting that you haven't done before. Unfortunately, La Scala is closed – it's off-season, so we won't be seeing any opera. Still, lots else to do. Don't forget your passport.

As if, Jeremy!!

Chloe met up with Karl mid-week at The King's Ransom. "I can't make the rave on Saturday night, Jeremy's taking me to Milan this weekend."

"Bloody hell, Chloe! I'm beginning to think you actually prefer being with him rather than me."

"Oh my poor Karlos .... are you getting a wee bit jealous?"

"No, I'm getting a wee bit pissed off."

"Well, if you were as good in bed as he is ..... and as for his supersized ...."

"Don't fuck with me, little bitch! I only agreed to you seeing him because you said you were going to find a way of relieving him of a substantial amount of cash, but so far you've done bugger all. In fact, bugger nothing!"

"Don't fret, big boy. The man we're going to visit is the same Nigerian that he told me about when we flew back from New York."

"The guy he did that shady property deal with?"

"Same one."

"Well, that seems to be his weakest link, so make bloody sure you get some dirt about the two of them that I can work with."

"At your command, Captain Karlos."

Chapter 25
Milano

Milan is the capital of Lombardy. Lombardy, a centre of culture since Renaissance times, is the most populous, productive and richest region in Italy. It is also the most industrial and polluted. There are times to avoid Milan – in summer the city is muggy and mosquito-riddled, in winter foggy. Neither extreme prevents millions of tourists from travelling there every year to observe the city that is the high priest of fashion and design in operation. The best time to visit is probably autumn, and as they flew over Milan there were few clouds in the sky on that late September day. The view was as clear as one was ever likely to get above Milan, and Jeremy was able to point out the Duomo and the Palazzo del'Arte.

Daniel's chauffeur was there to greet them. As they were driven to Daniel's apartment in mid-city in the luxurious BMW, Chloe realised, not for the first time, that Italy was a country where age, culture and climate came together with modernity to form a compelling and captivating whole. The thought filtered through her mind that if her wealth ever met her ambition, it was a country where she would want to spend a lot of time, perhaps even live for a while. Perhaps she could even start to learn Italian – that would certainly help her to understand those glorious operas a little better. She'd already picked up one word that Verdi used plentifully: *Maledizione.* Curses. It was nicely interchangeable with the rather common 'fuck it!', although Karl found it extremely pretentious.

The building itself was unostentatious, but, wow, the apartment! As they exited from the elevator directly into the entrance of the penthouse, which was bigger than Chloe's entire flat in Battersea, Daniel's Swedish wife Kristina and her three stunning young children were there to greet the visitors. The children, all under the age of ten, had never previously seen Jeremy with a woman of any age, so they were amazed to see such a young woman with their father's friend. Then the youngest, Paula, really put her foot in it when in all innocence she asked, "Is Uncle Jeremy your daddy?" Poor Kristina for once in her life was too embarrassed to speak, other than to say, "I hope you're hungry, because lunch is ready."

As Chloe looked around the apartment with its modernist Swedish furniture, its Danish kitchen, and its tasteful artwork, she began to appreciate what life could be like if one was unimaginably wealthy. As Daniel and Kristina were. As Jeremy was. Never having to ask the price of anything. You could have anything you wanted, go anywhere you chose.

Chloe, in those first fleeting moments, was being presented with a snapshot of the difference, the vast chasm that existed between Clapham Junction and Milan. Every single item in the apartment smacked of class, bled discreet, tasteful wealth.

There was however one thing she could not see anywhere – not on the furnishings, not on their clothes - a designer label. Or if there were any, they were very discreet. They did not scream, 'We are here, look at us!' It dawned on her that where she came from, a big label - whether on your sweater and jeans, your watch, your bag or your shoes, whether Abercrombie & Fitch, Burberry or Polo - was a sign that you were on the rise, that you were aspirational, that you could afford better than Zara or H&M. Yet here, where everything oozed good taste, not a thing was labelled with the interlinked Gs of Gucci or Versace's gorgon badge, or Louis Vuitton – just the pure understated elegance of the elite. Quiet luxury, the luxury of George and Amal Clooney, of Gwyneth Paltrow. These were the products of Lombardy designer Max Mara and the legendary Bottega Veneta, goods that spoke of quality and style rather than through brash logos.

And Chloe liked it. More than that, she craved it.

Lunch was taken on the *terrazza*, from where the enormous Duomo was in full view. Daniel's Nigerian chef, Abifoluwa, was a young woman who had decided that her traditional Lagos fare might be a tad too hot for her guests and had reverted to more traditional local dishes. The *risotto alla Milanesi* was executed with all the skill of a top-grade local chef and was accompanied by a ruby-red Barolo and followed by a perfectly ripened Tallegio cheese. When Chloe sniffed the formaggio platter, she nearly returned the risotto, but was brave enough to taste the cheese and found it wonderfully fruity in flavour.

As was his way, Jeremy was quick to praise. "Thank you, Abi, I've been telling Chloe about your creative ability in the kitchen, and that was right up there with your best." Chloe thought that *creating* food sounded a whole lot better than simply *making* lunch, and definitely in a different league to microwaving, as she prepared most of her meals.

The patio was bathed in glorious sunlight, blessed by a light breeze. Abi brought out the coffee that she served with her home-baked biscotti, as delicious as everything else. The two men then withdrew to discuss a business matter or two, and Chloe and Kristina could just pick up snatches of their conversation:

" .... grateful for your help ... ... saved my Barcelona man a heap of ... ... "

"Those Spanish bastards never knew what hit ...."

" ..... thinking of selling the Roses apartment. This squatter business is getting too much ....."

"..... don't like involving your father."

"His men enjoy breaking the odd ....."

Realising that the men needed to talk in private, Kristina suggested to Chloe that a visit to the jewel in the crown of Milan's magnificent shopping malls was a good idea and they should go and explore the Galleria Vittorio Emanuele, a pleasant walk away.

"Daniele has told me to give you *carte blanche* to buy whatever you want today" said Kristina, "It's all on him, and believe me, he can afford it."

"No way, Kristina, I'm happy to look, but I won't be spending anybody else's money, that's just not my way." Ha! Not much it wasn't, but she would have to curb her baser instincts on this occasion. *Maledizione!!*

It wasn't until they went into their final store, Dolce & Gabbana, that Kristina persuaded Chloe to try on a lilac cashmere sweater that, if one believed in such things, was heaven-made for Chloe. Even though Chloe insisted she did not want to have it, Kristina paid for the sweater as Chloe was changing back into her own gear.

"Understand something, Chloe, Daniele thinks the world of Jeremy – he's my husband's moral compass. This little gift to you will give Daniele enormous pleasure. You look absolutely gorgeous in it. Just wear it in good health and don't think any more about it."

Chloe flung her arms around this woman's petite shoulders, a woman she had met only two hours earlier but knew was already a friend.

As they sat down for coffee in one of the chi-chi cafeterias, coffee that was simply heavenly, she asked Kristina how she and Daniel had met.

"We were both students at Columbia in New York at the time. He was a senior, I was a sophomore. We were both writing articles for the student newspaper. Daniele was concerned with business matters, and I was the international affairs correspondent. Both of us being foreigners, we kind of gravitated to each other. Not all white girls were willing to pair up with a black guy, but being Swedish and very liberal, I didn't think twice. All I saw was a very decent and kind man, respectful of me. I quickly realised he was also ambitious and determined, and the cherry on the top, which you may have observed yourself, is that he's very handsome.

"Even when he told me about his father, I wasn't put off. He'd already changed his name, so I knew he had no intention of joining the family business. We got married in Stockholm, and I can say with my hand on my heart I've never regretted it for a moment. OK, so that's our story, what about you? Have you got anyone special?"

Chloe was about to tell her about Karl, but remembered that discretion was required and answered, "No one of note."

When they got back to the apartment, the men had finished their discussions, and it was champagne time. Of course, that put everyone in good spirits, or perhaps more accurately, good spirits in everyone. As they sat on the terrace looking down on the old city, Daniel and Chloe started to chat.

"When we first met, I thought you were from America," mused Chloe.

"You mean I don't have a Nigerian accent? That's because I was a student in America and not many people could understand my pronunciation. So I learned to adapt, and found it advantageous in a predominantly white society."

"I've never been to Africa, I'd love to. Until I met Jeremy, I'd only ever been out of England once, to Amalfi."

"Ha, you picked the most beautiful spot in the world to begin. Bad planning! I'm afraid Nigeria is rather different. Can be a culture shock to you Westerners, but I love to return there. Much of the country is desert and savannah plains, but we also have huge rainforests and waterfalls. We have the world's largest diversity of butterflies, and animals in abundance. Have you ever heard of the hyena men?"

"I've heard of hyenas, aren't they a bit repulsive, eating carcasses and all that?"

"Well, they may not be your average house pet, but in the north, a group of people have learned to tame them and keep the creatures in their homes. Hyena dung and saliva are used in medicinal remedies."

Once again Chloe managed to restrain herself from throwing up.

Daniel continued. "These hyena men make their living from showing them off at festivals and parades. They appear alongside the snake charmers, drummers and dancers, and children are encouraged to pet them."

"Yuck - isn't that kind of like dangerous?"

"Hyenas are known to attack livestock but don't generally attack humans, although I'm sure in Jeremy's case they'd make an exception. He'd make a good meal."

He ducked as Jeremy flung a napkin in his direction. They all watched as the napkin sailed over the balcony wall and fluttered its path to the pavement below, spiralling like a kite in the breeze.

"You're next, Daniel!"

Chloe couldn't help thinking that Jeremy was unlikely to be able to push anybody over anything, but then she had never heard of Krav Maga.

The day was to get even better. When they went out to for dinner that evening – the destination was a surprise, Kristina whispered - it was an experience that Chloe would not quickly forget. Chef Abi had left earlier that afternoon and, when the adults arrived, was putting the finishing touches to a meal on board Daniel's yacht on Lake Maggiore, a one-hour drive from Milan. Sunset while circumnavigating the lake on a fifty-foot cabin cruiser with all mod cons, a view of the Alps, eating lobster linguini and being serenaded by a local guitarist - how much better could it get? Did Chloe give Karl even the slightest thought? No chance. He could not have been further from her mind. Did she feel comfortable in the presence of a man twice her age and less than handsome, with a couple halfway between them in years? *Assoluto*, as Kristina would frequently say.

When she fell asleep on Jeremy's shoulder returning to Milan in Daniel's Maserati, it seemed the most natural thing in the world to be doing. Yet, when they got back to the Milanese apartment, it was separate bedrooms once more, and if she was honest with herself, she was beginning to wish it wasn't. Not for the sex, just to give something back to him, something he didn't know he needed.

The following morning, another surprise. As she sat with Daniel admiring the view from the terrace, he asked her if she was interested in football. Caught slightly off guard, she responded "Yeah, my boyfriend - I mean my ex-boyfriend - used to play professionally. Why do you ask?"

"I have a hospitality box at the San Siro, and it just happens that AC Milan are playing Inter Milan this afternoon – the local derby. I've managed to twist Jeremy's arm sufficiently hard to agree to the two of you joining us." Chloe leapt up and gave him a huge hug, and after that she hugged Jeremy. She knew that for him to attend a football match would be three hours of his life wasted. Yet, in the event, he and she both enjoyed the game enormously: she, because it was an unusually high-scoring game played in the most atmospheric stadium in Italy, he because he took simple pleasure in seeing her lapping up an experience that only his largesse could have brought her way.

Before they left that evening, Daniel handed her his business card - "If you ever need anything, you know where to find me" - and she suddenly remembered what her mission was in the first instance.

She texted both Jeremy and Daniel to thank them and Kristina for a wonderful weekend and received a courteous response from Kristina saying how much they in turn had enjoyed her company and youthful exuberance.

Chapter 26
Chloe Pulls the Plug

After she returned to work, Chloe's mind, unusually for her, went into overdrive. For the first time in her life, she felt the icy prickles of conscience. Was she really prepared to shaft Jeremy? For that matter, was it even necessary to shaft him? She knew that he had grown very fond of her. She felt intuitively that were she ever really in need of money, all she had to do was to mention it to him and her needs would be instantly met. So why take the low road when the high road was so much easier and a great deal safer? And the worst thing of all was that she really, really liked Jeremy, and he asked nothing from her except her company.

When she next met up with Karl, she told him that Daniel had given her his card, but what followed was a kick in the guts for Karl. Chloe told him she had changed her mind about the whole venture.

"I can't do it, Karl, I can't bring myself to steal from this man who has been so incredibly kind to me. He's become like an uncle to me."

Karl went quiet for a few seconds before he responded. "I was worried that might happen. Can't we just finish this job? I promise never to involve you again."

I'm really sorry, Karl, but I'm out."

Karl said nothing, but when she got up to go to the ladies', she did not see him open her bag and remove Daniel's card. Before she returned, it had been photographed and replaced.

Well aware to her occasional cost that he had an explosive temper, she was expecting him to be furious. But no angry outburst, no threats. Just calm.

"Been thinking about you and your fat uncle. I thought we had a deal, but if you want out, that's ok. Seems a pity, but no harm done."

He signalled to the bartender to top up their Jägermeisters. Had she thought for a second that he was now even more determined than ever to nail the fat old bastard, as Karl insisted on describing Jeremy, she would have headed straight for Jeremy's penthouse. But she did not know. The only feeling she was sure about was that, at that moment, she did not want to be with Karl. She could not bring herself to go back with Karl to his none too stylish studio flat, pleading tiredness after the weekend. He did not seem to mind.

The next few days were the most miserable that Chloe could remember experiencing for a very long time. She neither saw nor spoke to Karl. Not that she didn't want to - she missed his bright company, his carefree attitude, most of all his body up against her and inside her. She missed being with

Luke and her sister, their companionship. She knew she still liked Karl, but that seemed to be as far as it went. She realised that what she felt for him was companionship and lustful sex, but certainly not love.

On the other hand, what she felt for Jeremy was something entirely different. She was no longer aware of his unattractiveness and particularly not of his age, but so aware of his kindness. She had developed so much respect for the sharpness of his judgment, his wide cultural range, his sophisticated understanding of life. She wished she were more like him. Thus far he had given her so much, more than she could have expected, and had asked for nothing more than a smile in return. How could she possibly think of taking advantage, no, worse than that, stealing from him?

He had become to her what she had been seeking all her life: a father.

As things turned out, however, she heard very little from Jeremy over the next couple of weeks, other than to say he was extremely busy, occupied with getting the newly purchased company into shape.

She began to feel extremely lonely and alone, and phoned Karl to see if they could meet up again. He didn't seem to be pissed off with her in any way and was quite happy to come over to her apartment. To her relief, not a single thing was said about the abandoned project, and Jeremy's name fell out of their conversation. They slept together, and she remembered why she had liked him in the first instance. Whatever she might think of Karl's morality, he certainly knew how to find his way around her body. Normal life resumed.

For her, but not for Karl.

Chapter 27
Cybercrime

Whatever money was left that Karl had acquired courtesy of *Glorious Return* had been frittered away on less cooperative or responsive horses, and he began to realise that he needed to make a move against Jeremy. Not just Jeremy. Daniel too. And to do it immediately.

The entire property scene had also changed, not necessarily for the better. It had seen a rise in self-employed estate agents and a shift in the way that properties were being marketed online – less static images, more slick tour videos, and a growing number of sales being made on social media. They were shaking up London's property scene. At the forefront of this change was a new breed of property influencers: young, entrepreneurial, ambitious, and in touch with their vast audiences. They were the *propinfluencers*. Karl had every one of these attributes -he was charming, slick, and avaricious. It was all about the money. Social media was his playground. The scene was tailor-made for someone of his skill-set. Had Karl even the slightest desire to join the working classes, this was an area where he would probably have done well for himself if he was prepared to work reasonably and honestly. He wasn't. In any case, he was obsessed about teaching a fat ugly bastard a lesson.

Even though Karl had been just an average footballer, fate had dealt him a lousy hand when his injury put an end to his footballing career. Retired footballers develop antipathy to regular jobs that suit neither their personalities nor lifestyle. Sit in an office? Untenable. Become a tv football pundit? Get on to the entertainment circuits telling stories about memories of other footballers? Fine if you were sufficiently well known (Karl was not) and had a good football cv (Karl did not.)

He remembered an old aphorism - it is not the cards you are dealt, it is how you play them. He had played that lousy hand as well (if not as honestly) as he could and had made a fair bit of money, but it had not ended well. Worse, what was left of it he dared not access for some years. So, what you did was live on whatever capital you had earned during your active career, try to increase it by gambling, especially at the races, and enjoy hobbies such as fishing, a pastime which allowed much time for thinking. Karl spent his time fishing - and thinking.

Now he was after bigger fish, and as far as he could see, Jeremy and Daniel were shark-size.

An area where Karl was way above the common herd was in extracting secrets from computers. There were very few occasions when he had attempted to hack into someone's computer that, with patience, he had not been successful. In the past, he had managed on occasion to arrange some transfers from gullible bank account holders into his own, and at that time the risk of detection was not that great. But things were getting tougher, people were demanding greater controls by the banks. Karl did not fancy another stretch in one of Her Majesty's guest houses, so that avenue had come to an end, at least until his methods and skills improved. And improving they were. He needed to plan this operation very carefully.

Another avenue he considered he might follow, not to put too fine a point on it, was blackmail. Extortion. He liked the word 'extortion' more than 'blackmail'. He thought it perfectly reasonable to take money from someone who had been naughty (in this case, he thought, some two) and put it to use for a much more needy and worthy cause. Not that anything that the two had done was blatantly dishonest, but if their earlier property deal came to light, it would bring them to the attention of the authorities, somewhere they would definitely not wish to be going. Nor would they wish to have their hitherto untarnished reputations sullied. A million quid from each would not be too high a price for them to pay to stay clean.

However, the more he thought about it, the more he realised this was not a good idea if it could be avoided. Blackmailing someone was akin to assault; it smacked too much of criminal extortion, whereas what he wanted to involve himself with was wealth redistribution. Furthermore, were he silly enough to get caught, the prison sentences for blackmail were considerably longer than for cybercrime. Nevertheless, he did not exclude blackmail for starters. This would give him money to live on, but he was after bigger fish.

Cybercrime was all the rage, the *mode du jour,* practised by governments, admired by those who weren't smart enough to indulge in it themselves. Spiteful but clever stuff, and only the wealthy suffered. In the meantime, stick to what you're good at, Karl, and what you know is the world of computer fraud.

. Now that he had the names of the companies involved in the earlier deal *(thank you, my darling Chloe!),* it should not be too difficult to locate exact details of this and perhaps other transactions. Good honest research was required. Well, the research would be honest; what he planned to do with the data ... not gentlemanly conduct. From previous experience, he knew that the process of finding the information he wanted could take anything from days to months and, based on what little he had been able to glean thus far, it was more likely to be months.

He would need to set up a new bank account in a country that would not be co-operative in making shady transactions known to inquiring busybodies. The Cayman Islands sounded just the ticket. He considered having to fly there. He thought briefly of inviting Chloe to join him, but she had opted out of the project and would not approve of his plans. On further reflection, however, he concluded that unless he could make progress with his hacking, such a trip would be a huge drain on already limited existing resources. So, until there was clear-cut need, he might have to wait to see how things panned out with his project.

What of his relationship with the gorgeous Chloe? Oddly for a man who was extremely self-confident, green shoots of jealousy were rearing their little heads. She was having such a jolly time with the old fart, going here, there, and everywhere. Where had they been so far? New York, Milan, Santa Fe. No, not yet Santa Fe, but Chloe was talking lots about it. No doubt, other places would follow. It was beginning to get on his tits. Well, if that's the way you want to play it, babe, so be it.

Karl, like most men, suffered from one inherent disability - insecurity. Was she turning off him because he was inherently unstable, and sold herself to this fat merchant who was lousy with money? He tried to rationalise that what she was doing was better than involvement with a young man, but when he thought of that bastard pawing her (even though she said he was not), the thumbscrews tightened on his guts and the red mist floated. He could not shake from his mind the possibility that she didn't want him with all his manhood and fire in his belly; instead, she seemed to be going for this old heavyweight who could buy her diamonds and mink. The tart. The fucking little whore. Don't get too fond of him, Chloe, or his bank balance won't be the only thing I'll be hitting.

Then a semblance of reason prevailed. She wasn't the only pebble on the beach, although she was by far the brightest.

His and Chloe's future relationship would be restricted to clubs and beds, and if it became necessary, he would just have to limit the latter, but only after he had taken the old fart to the cleaners. Not too quickly though – he needed the information she was providing, meagre though it was.

What data did Karl have to hand so far? Not a great deal but enough to get started. Jeremy's name and address; the nature of his business (property); a property acquisition in Aldgate that was sold a month after purchase; a residential property purchase in Kilburn; the name of Jeremy's bank; his involvement with the Royal Opera House. He also had Daniel Odenfemji's name and address, and his involvement with the Aldgate deal. As far as detail was concerned, little more, but he could now discern the head of a nail, a nail that could be driven deeper and deeper until the wall cracked. He did not think it would be an easy nail to hammer (he was correct in that assumption), but a challenge that was within his capabilities, however long it took. How wonderful is the Internet, he thought, where information about anybody who was somebody could be accessed if you knew how to go about it.

He knew.

Chapter 28

Santa Fe

Chloe had indeed been talking about Santa Fe. She knew little about it except that it featured in a lot of old western movies that involved Mexicans and native-American Indians. When she googled Sante Fe, three things seemed to stand out: Cormac McCarthy, Georgia O'Keeffe, and the Sante Fe opera house. Chloe didn't read much, but a name she knew was that of Cormac MCarthy, because she had seen and loved the film 'No Country for Old Men' based on one of his books. Georgia O'Keeffe's name meant nothing to her, until (googling again) she saw the wonderful landscapes and flowers this woman had painted. It was the third attraction that knocked her socks off. She realised that even for a girl from the Peabody Estate in Clapham Junction, she could see the addiction that opera and living life high on the hog was becoming – who'da thought?

Another flight to New York where this time the stop was very brief. Waiting for Jeremy was a 'realtor' with some papers that required signature. Another day, another deal. Then, the private jet refuelled, a six-hour flight to Santa Fe where they were to spend three nights. It had not been easy for Chloe to arrange this time off from work, but when she explained to her boss what she would be missing if she was not excused, her employer had said, "Chloe, you deserve your lucky break. Go have a great time!" Lucky she was. A great time? Is going to see and hear Madame Butterfly while seated in one the most unusual opera houses around not great?

The Santa Fe Opera House is essentially an open-air arena, but with a covering roof to protect spectators from the elements. The stage too was covered, but with a wide-open backdrop that allowed a view of the surrounding scrubland and hills, and most awesome of all, the gradually darkening sky - sunset in all its magnificent red and gold glory. Just to add to the aura, small bolts of lightning could be seen exploding in the distance to the gentlest rumble of thunder.

Puccini's Butterfly proved to be even better than her expectations. The threatening real-life storm outside was in total harmony with the shitshow that awaited the poor young Japanese geisha mother – it sent shivers through her body. When Cio-Cio-San plunged her concealed knife into her guts, Chloe could feel the pain in her own. The rainstorm never happened, except for the trickle of wetness that fell from her eyes. She kept pinching herself – what had she done to deserve this!

The best was still to come, and it arrived in the form of a concert the following night by John Fogerty, the singer/guitarist /songwriter who had formerly been with Credence Clearwater Revival. Jeremy had not given the slightest hint that they would be attending this gig. He hadn't booked this just for Chloe, though. Much as his musical life was vested in opera and the classics, there were a few rock albums in his collection, and these included CCR and The Byrds - yes, Jeremy liked country rock! The gig turned out to be one of the highlights of Chloe's life to date, and when they got to attend the after-party and chatted to the musician, she offered a silent prayer to whichever deity had prevented her from following through with her ill-considered scheme.

Earlier that day, they had explored the myriad of small galleries that seemed to outnumber the coffee shops, and there was no shortage of the latter. Jeremy suggested she choose something she would like to take home as a souvenir, and she selected a signed photographic print by Ansel Adams. Jeremy congratulated her on her choice, saying Adams was one of the world's greatest photographers. Then she looked at the price tag and gulped: $1,200. "No way, Jeremy, I couldn't afford that!"

"Don't be silly, young lady - it's a gift from me and will probably go up nicely in value. In any case, it's chicken feed compared to what I'm about to spend at our next stop." The next stop of course was the Georgia O'Keeffe Museum, where Jeremy had come to collect a limited signed print of an original work by the venerated artist, one that would cost more than Chloe could earn in a lifetime. She realised that this, and not the visit to the opera, was his main reason for visiting the small but delightful city built entirely of terracotta-coloured adobe houses.

Jeremy's world of art, music and gastronomy was clearly seeking increasing space in her mind, and she was open to receiving it from this gentle, well-mannered benefactor. Chloe mentioned nothing of the trip's purchases to Karl, whom she sensed was becoming less than thrilled about her involvement with the fat old bastard, as Karl so unkindly referred to Jeremy. She was sensible enough not get annoyed, but realised she was liking his boorish behaviour and lack of manners less and less. Whatever benefits Karl brought to their relationship, mostly delivered when she was horizontal, they definitely did not include cultural upgrading.

Chapter 29
A Breakthrough

Karl had spent every minute of her absence abroad glued to his computer but thus far had come up with almost nothing. It was becoming increasingly clear to him that his prey were not average punters. They were either highly skilled computer boffins in their own right (unlikely) or able to afford brilliant technicians who were. The system's fibre optics were bullet-proof closed circuit and would never be used for ordering goods from a superstore, that was for sure. They were completely dedicated to preserving their own impenetrability and integrity. A less motivated criminal than Karl might have thrown in the towel, but he was obsessed with making a break-through, no matter how long it took.

The breakthrough, when it arrived a few weeks later, came not in the way Karl had expected. He had been trying every possible technological avenue and technique but had come up with nothing, but the card of fortune that was about to flip for him had nothing to do with technology. It was to do with the Daily Mail.

As one might expect, Karl was not an avid newsreader. He was not a newsreader at all. What was happening in

Venezuela or Vietnam or even Vauxhall were matters of complete indifference to him. The only reason he kept the Daily Mail app on his phone was to access football stories and information and tips from racing pundits. Then, searching for some information about a possible takeover bid of Charlton Athletic by an American baseball team owner, Karl followed a link to the business section.

There, sitting just below the article dealing with yet another failed football club putsch, was a heading: "Jeremy Lawson's Aida Property Holdings Bids to Buy Historic New York Landmark."

The article that followed described a forty-room building in downtown New York where an eccentric art-dealer had lived with his wife and two sons. The thirty rooms that were not occupied by the family were filled with a treasure trove of paintings, manuscripts and sculptures accumulated over the past fifty years. When the patriarch died, his sons sent the contents of those thirty rooms for auction. The money realised (not to mention the value of the property up for sale) was sufficient to ensure that neither the two young men, nor their children, nor their future children's children even unto the fifth generation would ever have to work a day in their lives.

The bid for the property was the document Jeremy had signed in that brief stopover in New York on the way to Santa Fe, and the article continued by describing the success of Aida Property Holdings over many years, mentioning in passing how Jeremy had chosen its name. Were it to acquire the

Lansdowne-Burlington building in New York, it would become the jewel in Aida's crown.

While growing up in South Africa, Karl could not have avoided being aware of the ubiquitous Aida Estate Agency, a highly successful property vendor named after its eponymous founder. By sheer coincidence it was also the name Jeremy had chosen for his property company. From where Jeremy's company had got its name was a matter of complete indifference to Karl, but details of its dealings were not.

So Karl began to explore Aida Property Holdings UK, or as its acronym was referred to by others with some amusement, APHUK. He found something very interesting.

Chapter 30
The Prostate Gland

On his return from Santa Fe, being as involved as he was trying to push through the purchase of the New York Lansdowne-Burlington building, Jeremy was not focusing on his bladder or prostate. The tablets that had been prescribed for him seemed to be doing what it said on the box. He was peeing with good flow and without discomfort, sleeping better for it. Perhaps it had just been a timeous warning sign. That was until Dr Victor Smythe telephoned.

"My dear man, do you realise it's been eight months since you last visited me? Are you deliberately avoiding me?"

"Not at all, Victor. It's just been an incredibly hectic period business-wise and I guess I took my eye off the ball."

"Time to remedy that. Can you make Thursday at 3?"

"If I must."

"You must. By the way, how is the young lady friend who has got Covent Garden tongues wagging?"

Jeremy felt his face reddening.

"No substance to those rumours, I can assure you. Mere prattle from idle tongues. We're just friends, Victor."

"I never thought I'd hear that hoary old chestnut coming out of your mouth! The rumours must then be true. Who'd have thought ..."

At the earliest opportunity he dropped in at the Harley Street Laboratory to have his urine and blood tests. Two days later Dr Victor Smythe conducted a repeat examination, and once more apologised for having to insert his gloved finger into Jeremy's rectum. On this occasion however it was not a brief foray, and when the finger was removed, the gloves disposed and the hands washed, he turned to face Jeremy. "Hmm, old chap, the hardening of the left lobe of the prostate is still quite large, possibly even larger, I'm afraid. Unfortunately, I can now feel a definite swelling in the outer capsule of epithelium surrounding the gland. I would expect to find this in men in their eighties but not in their early sixties. I'm concerned that it has developed quite so quickly since our last inspection. I've also had a look at the results of your tests and unfortunately, they do show blood in the urine. Your PSA reading has also increased."

Jeremy blanched but remained calm. "Cancer?"

"Looking very much like it. What we don't know however is whether it is benign or malignant. What I want to suggest is that we do what we call a TRUS, a trans-rectal ultrasound scan, where a surgeon will pass a rod up your rectum via your anal sphincter and produce an image from the sound waves. The rod will also have a fine needle attached, which will penetrate the tumour for a biopsy that will tell us if the cells are cause for concern."

"And if they are?"

"We'll cross that bridge when we come to it. If worse comes to worst and you do require surgery, you'll end up without a prostate, but I'm probably right in thinking it's not been much use to you anyway. Unless . . ." He paused, smiling mischievously at Jeremy, "You're not planning on having children, are you, or is there something you're not telling me? You know, son and heir, that sort of thing?"

"When did you become a joker, Victor?"

"Just asking."

"Seeing that you're 'just asking', let me tell you why I find this young lady's companionship more uplifting than that of my contemporary colleagues and their wives. They - actually, I'm not even sure who 'they' are - they say it's good to talk. Maybe. Sometimes it's interesting; more often than not, it's not. If you're going to be holding a conversation with someone, it doesn't do a lot for your spirit if what you get is an organ recital: 'My guts won't work, haven't crapped in three days', or, 'my throat's aching, I don't know if it's from spending so much time on the phone or if I've got this virus', or 'my legs are cramping from sitting so much.' Those poor dears, have they tried some exercising besides going to the fridge? Do they really need to rabbit on for 45 minutes about how their sons don't phone them? When I'm with them, too often all I really want to do is find a very sharp knife to slit my throat painlessly. Or better, still, theirs.

"Well, Victor, I don't get any of this from young Chloe. I get brightness and cheer, optimism instead of cynicism. She doesn't come within a mile of my intellect, but after an evening in her company I feel less aged than I have become or probably always have been. Does than make sense?"

Victor just stared at him. Was this Jeremy speaking?

Two days later, Jeremy presented himself at another Harley Street clinic for the scan, which was carried out under a very light general anaesthetic. When he awoke, he was pleasantly surprised to find that, despite the surgeon's foray up his backside, he was experiencing no discomfort whatsoever, and three hours later he was back in his apartment sipping cognac and listening to Beethoven.

His cell phone buzzed. It was Victor. "Bad news and good news, my friend. The bad news is it that we have picked up early malignancy. The good news is that as far as the pathologist can tell it does not appear to have spread. So, dear boy, it's the butcher's block for you for a partial prostatectomy next week, and hopefully that will be the end of it."

Jeremy smiled ruefully. "I hope not the end of me."

Over the next couple of days, he made four phone calls.

The first was to Daniel.

"Daniel, we need to meet up in the next couple of days. Unfortunately, I have developed cancer of the prostate, not too seriously, I hope. I will need you to take over the Lansdowne-Burlington negotiations and I need to brief you on the current state of play."

"I will be with you by tomorrow evening."

Daniel, as requested, flew to London the following day. He tried not to appear downbeat during the seven hours of intense discussion. It was difficult to remain impassionate, however, and before leaving, Daniel put his arm around the older friend who had become his mentor and confidant and said, "If you're planning to die on me, I'll send my father's men to kill you."

The second phone call Jeremy made, as a matter of courtesy, was to his solicitor. He informed Sir Christopher of the doctor's diagnosis and told him he wished to maintain his will as it was. The lawyer, as instructed, did nothing. What he thought was a story rather different. In his eyes, what he saw was something that he had seen many times before: the age-old story of a wealthy older man being swept off his feet by the apparent adoration of a pretty young naif. It rarely ended well.

The third call was to Chloe. She burst into tears and, barely able to talk, promised to visit him after his operation. Chloe called Karl to tell him the news. To her surprise, he was very sympathetic, and this pleased her, especially when he said he hoped Jeremy would be around for a good while longer. She did not realise that Karl needed time to find the keys he was seeking, and if blackmail was to be essential to his plan, he also needed to have a live Jeremy.

The fourth call was to arrange an urgent appointment with the head of Urology at University College Hospital to whom he had been referred by Victor. As it turned out, when he visited the eminent professor, the medical man was the bearer of good news.

"I've had a good look at your MRI scans, Mr Lawson. It appears that although you do have prostate cancer, it is a relatively small mass and very easily accessible. Rather than subjecting you to open surgery, what I propose is to carry out is a procedure known as HIFU, High Intensity Focused Ultrasound. I'll try to explain it without getting too technical. HIFU is essentially a minimally invasive soundwave-based treatment using a pair of high-energy ultrasound beams that heat-targets areas of the prostate, destroying cancer cells while leaving the rest of the prostate and its surrounding structures alone. HIFU is performed under general anaesthetic in a single treatment session usually lasting about two hours and will allow you to leave the hospital within 90 minutes of completion. The only downside is that you will have to urinate via a catheter for a couple of weeks while the swelling goes down after the operation. How does that sound to you?"

"Aside from the catheter, that sounds like the best news I've had all week!"

When Jeremy awoke after the anaesthetic, although still in a haze, he could make out two familiar faces standing there: Victor and Chloe. It was Chloe who took his hand, but Victor who spoke: "Good news, chum; the surgeon is confident that he removed all the malignant tissue, and we'll have you up and around in no time flat. Now we need to let you rest."

As the two visitors walked into the corridor, the elderly doctor paused and looked at Chloe. "I can see why Jeremy thinks so well of you, young lady. Take good care of him, will you."

"I definitely will, Doctor, I promise."

The promise was kept, and for the next three weeks, Chloe was a constant visitor to Jeremy's apartment. How thankful she was that she had opted out of the project. She also saw a lot of Karl during those weeks, his body providing much-needed balm to her concerned soul.

The pain Jeremy had expected turned out to be little more than mild discomfort. The catheter that had been inserted into his penis to allow him to urinate was far more of an irritant, and the catheter was determined to delay departure from that part of its host's body to which it had become accustomed. It was eventually removed by a male nurse, although that took two weeks longer than expected.

His personal trainer still came round daily, but the exercises were definitely less strenuous. Still, he made good progress and his life gradually returned to a revised version of normality.

Chapter 31
The Game Unfolds

The Lansdowne-Burlington building was finally added to his portfolio, and he and Daniel were able to devote full attention to planning its future development. They decided to employ an Anglo-Nigerian architect whose family stemmed from Lagos. Her name was Adaka Chukwu, and she had previously been employed by Daniel on several occasions. Jeremy frequently admired the thorough preparation and fine detail she put into her work. She was, as Daniel had always stated, rock-solid, and took no risks. Her brief was simply to prepare a feasibility study for a conversion of use from residential to commercial, stuff she did in her sleep. The appointment was widely reported in the New York state financial columns and online.

It was this liaison that looked like it might offer Karl the keys to the kingdom. Or so he hoped. Once again he was wrong. The deal was so above board that it made him feel angry and frustrated. He was not used to dead ends. There had to be a way through the impenetrable maze that didn't end in a brick wall ...

The computerised financial control system proved as unbreachable as ever. What Karl did not realise was that the very people he was tracking were beginning to track him. The more obsessed Karl was becoming, the more he was leaving clues, not about himself, merely the fact that both Jeremy and Daniel were becoming aware they were being targeted.

Daniel and Jeremy discussed this at one of their London meetings. Daniel was the first to react. "When we find these guys, they will regret the day they were born, I swear to it."

"What do you propose to do, Daniel?"

"Track. Identify. Dispose. I said I prefer not to have much to do with my father and his thugs, but they can occasionally be put to good use."

"Sounds good to me. I'll set my personal fraud squad rottweilers on the track as well to see if we can sniff them out."

The tracker was being tracked. Jeremy's minions were on the case. One again a slow, laborious process, but what anti-fraud boffins possess in abundance is patience. Step by step, bit by bit, byte by byte. But as was Karl's experience, they could only get up to a certain point where the trail seemed to evaporate into the ether.

Stalemate.

Karl also realised he was in danger and made the decision to get out while he could. He would have to find another way, perhaps a return to plan B. He was about to realise what Jeremy had learned those years before: needs must when the devil arrives. Necessity compelled.

A few months went by. Jeremy returned to his doctor for what he hoped would be his final prostate check-up, but the demeanour of Dr Victor Smythe was anything but encouraging.

"I'm sorry, Jeremy, but your PSA readings have started to rise again. I'm afraid to say it's not looking great. No need for panic stations, but we need to continue to monitor your condition very carefully. Let's see you in three months, and don't muck about this time, alright?"

Jeremy suddenly saw his mortality staring him in the face. He was not one who panicked, but this was not what he was hoping for. Was this news the harbinger of worse to come? Once again, he resolved to sort his affairs out so that nothing was unnecessarily left to the Receiver of Revenue, and there was one matter that might require attention in the near future: his state pension.

Jeremy was fully aware that in the event of his death, the not insubstantial pension he was receiving would die with him. There was only one way to prevent that happening and that was for his pension to pass to his spouse, but he was and had always intended to remain unmarried. Now, for the first time in his life there was a pertinent reason and a suitable candidate in the running. Chloe. Of course, she was not his spouse – not yet anyway. But if she were to marry him, even if the marriage was never consummated, she would not only inherit a substantial sum of money but a monthly pension that was substantially greater than her own earnings. He resolved to discuss this with her and would have done so had something far more pressing and concerning reared its extremely ugly head – a very black cloud.

Chapter 32
A Very Nasty Letter

In the old days when people sent real mail, one could gain an impression of what lay inside the envelope by the handwriting on it. The quality of the paper used also conveyed a message. Emails, on the other hand, were amorphous and bland. They all looked alike. It was not until you opened them that their purpose would be revealed. Thus, an email about a forthcoming sale would look exactly the same as one threatening your livelihood, until you pressed 'open.'

It's rare that you receive a letter that could genuinely change your life. When that email arrived, Jeremy was concerned. Very concerned indeed.

<jeremyLawson4596@gmail.com>

cc <daniel@odenfemji.net.ita>

Dear Mr Lawson

I have been following the course of your successful career for some time now, always with great admiration. International developer, generous philanthropist, patron of the arts: everything that one could aspire to be.

Rumour has it that your achievements and largesse have come to the attention of His Majesty's Government, and that shortly you may be able to prefix your name with that short but oh so respected title of SIR. Sir Jeremy Lawson - how sweetly that name rolls off the tongue! It has a real ring of class about it. And who is to say that, after your generous contributions to all those charities, you don't deserve such an honour.

Well, Mr Lawson, there are a small number of people who might say exactly that. I am one such person. Here is why I think you may not deserve to be honoured. As I said earlier, I've been following your career for a very long time, and I am aware of an event, in fact several events that took place in your early years as a developer. Activities, details of which would be of great interest to the tabloid press, details for which they would be prepared to pay substantial sums of money. Pursuits such as forcing certain individuals to leave their properties through physical coercion. Details that would cause tongues to cluck in high places and effectively ensure that you remain a common ordinary Mr Jeremy Lawson for the rest of your life.

Small beer, you might say, but it gets worse - I am referring to other activities such as MONEY LAUNDERING.

You see, Mr Lawson, I think laundering money for a notorious Nigerian crime ring is not a worthy contribution to the good name of this country. Not an activity that would bother an ordinary person such as myself but would almost certainly bother the afore-mentioned group of dignitaries who decide on the Honours List. Were such activities to become known to those lofty people, they might be tempted to reconsider whatever thoughts they were having, and perhaps the anticipated knighthood might never be realised.

Nor do I think that a certain highly regarded English bank would be happy either; nor for that matter a well-respected Nigerian gentleman. Oh, forgot to mention, I have also been following the career of your associate Mr Daniel Odenfemji. A career so far unblemished. He would not be happy if his relationship to a certain gentleman in an African country was to become common knowledge. Racketeering, prostitution, drug dealing, extortion by coercion, money laundering. Especially money laundering. Mr Odenfemji is not a British citizen and has to apply every five years to extend his residency permit. He would not be happy were this permit to be denied to him. Nor if his name too was smeared across the Daily Mail.

Now, just to reiterate, Jeremy, soon to be Sir Jeremy, I am not a vindictive man. I have no personal grudge against you, au contraire, only unbridled admiration. You absolute deserve whatever honours come your way - you've certainly earned them. My problem unfortunately is that I'm unemployed at present and extremely impecunious, whereas you on the other hand have rather a lot of money (almost all of it legitimately earned and properly taxed), although one must say that too much of it is being wasted on la dolce vita and gluttony.

As I said earlier, you are known to donate lavish amounts to charity. What I want to suggest is that you may wish to consider me a worthy charitable cause. I've hit hard times and the only asset I possess is my knowledge of your activities. Not a tangible asset but one that I can sell for a lot of dosh.

The only outstanding question is, who will be the buyer? The Daily Mail? The Sun on Sunday? Or those two nice guys Jeremy and Daniel? I'd so prefer it to be just the two of you.

I'm not a greedy person, but I know for sure that I can get a seven-figure sum for information to the gutter press. That's not in total, it's seven figures for each of you, and being the unfussy person I am, I will leave it to each of you to decide which seven figures.

I'm going to leave you to think about it for the next three days. Then I will write again to you and provide details of how the bank transfer is to be affected. You know what to do and how to do it. If the money is not then in my account within three days of my request, you will never hear from me again. But others will.

With kindest regards and unlimited respect,

Yours, ???

Without wishing to sound snobbish, you may be surprised that, considering Karl spent most of his time with the football fraternity, the language and tone of the letter was so upmarket, but you must remember that Karl had the benefit of a very good education, not least from his father. All a bit of a waste, you might be thinking. Slippery and oleaginous, had he ever been bitten by a poisonous snake, chances are it would not have been the reptile that survived. Simply, he was toxic.

Jeremy read the message, read it again. His heart began to beat that much faster, and his mouth went dry. But the worst thing of all was the message flashing across his brain, writ in capital letters, underlined and in bold. Even though it bore no name, he knew without a shadow of doubt who was behind this email. Directly or indirectly? Did it make a difference?

He phoned Daniel. Daniel arrived in his private jet six hours later and headed straight to Jeremy's apartment.

"Any idea who this might be, Jeremy? From my perspective, it's impossible to identify him. Literally thousands could link me to my father."

"I don't know specifically who this person is, but I am quite certain who provided his information."

"And he is .... ?"

"Not he – she. You know me well, Daniel. You know that I am circumspect beyond necessity. I'm ashamed to admit that the only person to whom I have ever disclosed any sort of description about my past is - - - Chloe." His voice faltered as he choked on his words. "It can only be Chloe. Looks very much like she is my Eve, even my Delilah. It looks like the underdog is trying to get the big bone."

Daniel was speechless. Was this possible? This man, who had shunned any form of contact with women, had his head been turned by this pretty, intelligent, but it must be said, common young woman? Chloe had never struck him as a gold-digger. Had she fooled them all – Jeremy, Daniel, Kristina?

Jeremy continued, "I don't have to tell you that we have been under attack financially by potential cyber-fraud hackers. I do not think that activity is unrelated to this letter. The only person, the ONLY person I have opened up to is Chloe, once when we were flying back from New York. I'm ashamed to say this but I think this is a sting and I may have been honey-trapped."

"You mean she was part of a set-up?"

"I am beginning to think that is precisely what has been going on."

"How are you going to deal with it?"

"I could confront her immediately, but she would just deny it. I need hard evidence. So, I'm going to do what I always do - carry out due diligence. Let me think about it."

"Well, think also that even if we pay him or her or them, there's not a thing we can do if they still want to sell to the press."

"I have no doubt that's exactly what would happen. But you know, what, little brother, we are both successful men, and we didn't become successful by being stupid. They are smart. We must be smarter. Just a game of chess."

Jeremy went into another room and returned about twenty minutes later.

"Okay, Daniel, I've just spoken to the man who carries out private investigations for me, and we've decided that first he's going to hack into her emails and calls – shouldn't be difficult – and then arrange for her to be tailed. Sorry if this sounds a bit gumshoe-ish, but if I'm going to confront Chloe, I need to be very sure of my facts. Meanwhile, let's play ball with this blackmailing douchebag."

Dear Sir

Please excuse the formality of this response, but I do not know your name. You certainly know mine! I'm afraid you've got me over a barrel. Actually, both Daniel and me. I can only admire your achievement! The sad thing is, had you approached me honestly and made me aware of your considerable talents in hacking and researching information, I would have been happy to employ you at a stonking great salary. Such irony, such a shame ....You could have been earning a million quid a year with me!

Anyway, in response to your proposal: I've discussed the matter with Daniel, and we have agreed that we will each pay you £1,000,010 (one million and ten pounds) - the extra £10 is to show we are generous at heart.

We do however only ask two things from you: We will require a little extra time to convert assets to cash, so say two weeks rather than the one week you suggest. The second is an irrevocable promise from you not to attempt to extort further contributions from us.

We await your positive reaction.

Sincerely, etc.

Karl's eyes lit up. This was going better than he had dreamed. He had not expected Jeremy to capitulate so comprehensively. He must really want that knighthood! Karl understood the request for extra time but hadn't thought of factoring interest into the equation. And as for 'no further contributions', it hadn't been in his mind, but it certainly was now. Thanks, ugly fat bastard!

The response was from a different email address.

Dear Sir Jeremy,

That title certainly has a ring to it! I found your note a trifle condescending. I'm not a hardened criminal and am not looking for more than a reasonable reward to save you from a great deal of embarrassment. I accept your request for an extra week's extension but must insist that for each extra day of that week my fees will go up at the rate of £50,000 per day. EACH. So, if my calculations are correct, and even if they're not, at the end of the second week, I will expect £1,350,000. Thereafter, an additional £100,000 / day. You can keep the extra £10 and use it for toilet paper.

I hereby give you an irrevocable promise not to seek further contributions to my wellbeing when the above-mentioned amounts are paid into my account. You will be notified of the exact details for the transfer, IBAN, a/c no., and precise time on day 14.

Do not fuck this up, or the Sir Jeremy event won't be happening!!!

The beauty of his scheme, Karl realised, was that Chloe would never ever get to know how he had obtained the windfall that was now guaranteed to come his way. There wasn't a chance that Jeremy would tell her how he had been fleeced, and even if he did, there would be nothing pointing to him as the perpetrator. He would simply explain it as reward for assisting in a lucrative football transfer.

He praised himself for the simplicity of his scheme. No bags stuffed with money to be collected from a busy car park or culvert. No police lying in wait. Just one quick milli-second electronic transfer to an account in the Caymans, divide the money into twenty batches to be transferred just as instantly to banks in Holland and Croatia that he could access at will, not like the money lying in Spain. No, this would be the simplest deal he had ever done. Quick. Clean.

Once the money was in the bank, he would divert his charm and energy to reclaiming the biggest prize of all – Chloe. Yes, he was well aware that her head had been turned by the generosity of her benefactor, but he still had one asset that the old man did not possess, and that asset lay not in a bank but in his Armani briefs. She had told him that Jeremy was suffering from prostate cancer that would soon render him incapable of travelling, and without that, what did Jeremy have to offer? Karl would be able to turn her head away from her loss by hiring a catamaran in Bali, Bora-Bora or the Maldives. He would even get Jeremy to fund these luxurious outings, because Karl would always retain hovering over Jeremy's head the sword of Damocles that was the threat of having the tycoon's reputation sullied and besmirched. As they said down Peckham way, bootiful!

Or should he even care what Chloe wanted? He was beginning to find her tiresome. If she wanted to spend time with a guy twice her age who couldn't even get his soldier to stand to attention, that was her problem. His was always up for it and he was definitely not short of places to station his soldier for a night's duty.

Chapter 33
Endgame

Peter Diddescroft was not a person you would notice in a crowd. In fact, he was not a person you would notice if he were the only other occupant in a lift. Yet, it was precisely that quality of invisibility, of not being there, that made Peter Diddescroft the effective gumshoe that he was. He had staked out people frequently in the past on behalf of Mr J Lawson, and, unbeknown to Daniel, had even tailed the Nigerian in the earliest days of his acquaintance with Jeremy. The habits and colleagues of a prospective partner required thorough investigation that was beyond the inspection of balance sheets. One could never be too careful.

The extremely unobtrusive Mr Diddescroft - the only thing unusual about him was his name - was a man with infinite patience. You had to have that quality to be able to sit in the coffee shop opposite Starlite Dental waiting for Chloe to emerge. Then to tail her to one or other of the many boutiques that she seemed to frequent with undiminished energy. To stand on the pavement while she visited her mother or her sister or other pretty friends. Finally, to follow her on the sixth night into the King's Ransom and observe her fling herself into the arms of a man that he knew instantly was the lowlife he was hoping to find.

He hovered around the couple as they moved though from lounge seat to bar, sufficiently close to catch the man's name - Karl; then a half hour later to overhear a waitron addressing the man as Mr Janssens. Finally, to follow 'him to her apartment and remain outside till both emerged the following morning. A man of infinite patience ...

His next step was to key in 'Karl Janssens' to his search engine. There it was: '*South African, ex-professional footballer, prison record for fraud*.'

Bingo!

As far as the information that he imparted to Jeremy was concerned, the one item that hurt Jeremy the most was that Karl had been a professional footballer. The thought of being in the company of a young woman who was literally sharing her bed with a footballer made him feel dirty. When he repeated this to Daniel, the Nigerian remembered Chloe's words to him as they sat on his terrace prior to going to the Milan football derby: "*Yeah, my boyfriend - I mean my ex-boyfriend - used to play professionally. Why do you ask?*" He reiterated this to his friend.

The ducks were beginning to fall into line.

Time to act. Time to commence the duck-shoot.

Jeremy remembered the lesson he had learned in chess: there were situations when one had to sacrifice a soldier or even an officer in order to improve one's position. Chloe - his queen - had to go, of that there was no question, but this move had to be done with cunning.

He dialled Chloe's number.

"Hullo, Chloe, Jeremy."

"Jeremy! How lovely to hear from you! I thought you had forgotten me."

"Little chance of that happening, my dear, just been rather busy. Listen, young lady, I'd like you to pop over my apartment, this evening if possible. Also, I have a friend who would love to see you."

"I bet it's Daniel!"

"You might be right, but whoever it is would not be happy if he went home not having spent an evening with you."

Chloe's mind began to buzz – was Jeremy saying Daniel fancied her? Well, she already knew that. But was Jeremy actually setting it up for them? Improbable - but not impossible. You never knew with men.

"Unfortunately, I'm busy this evening, but how about tomorrow night?"

"Fine, that might even be better. 8pm?"

"Can't wait. Is Kristina with Daniel?"

"I didn't say it was Daniel, but whoever it may be is on his own."

"Send him my love."

"Oh, and by the way, I want to tell you about an important change I have made in my will."

"What is it, Jeremy ?"

"You'll have to wait till tomorrow."

"No, tell me!"

"Tomorrow evening."

Chloe was intrigued. His will? What important changes? Did these possibly involve her? Was he about to tell her he planned to leave something for her? If so, this would not be likely to happen for a while - his prostate was in good condition as far as she was aware. No, it couldn't be – surely he would be leaving everything to charity as he always said he would. Or to Daniel. But if he was leaving his money or some of it to Daniel, it might pay her to ensure that their friendship became even closer. She regretted having said she couldn't get there that evening, but it would look poor if she said she'd changed her mind. And then again, maybe she was getting her hopes up for nothing. Maybe he just wanted her to witness his signature - cool it, girl, he doesn't owe you anything. But just maybe...

Jeremy smiled wryly at Daniel. "I wonder if she realises she has just cost me £50,000 by this delay?"

Daniel appreciated the irony.

Jeremy slept fitfully that night. He wasn't sure what was bothering him most: his ever-tightening prostate in his groin, the pain of sadness in his heart, or the bitterness of betrayal in his mouth. The next twenty hours or so would be telling, and he was not looking forward to it.

Chloe, on the other hand, was sleeping soundly. Karl had been unusually cheerful a few hours before as he told her of a deal he was working on that was about to come to fruition. Karl was not forthcoming with the details, and Luke did not seem to know much about this. Whatever, just about every deal Karl had been working on had not reached a satisfactory ending, and this one wasn't likely to either. That, thought Chloe, was how it was with Karl. Best not to think about and just enjoy his high spirits. Back at his flat, a line of cocaine had fuelled his levels of testosterone, and his lovemaking had been more passionate than for some time. Karl's hairy arms were enfolding her body as she dropped off into an easy sleep. Had she but known ...

Chapter 34
The Endgame Ends

At exactly 8pm Jeremy's doorbell rang – being a dental receptionist, Chloe understood the value of punctuality. As she had become accustomed to doing, she had dressed with great taste and had not forgotten to bring a mini-bouquet. Feeling in a really great mood, she gave each man a warm hug. Not for the first time, she thought to herself that she would really enjoy a roll in the hay with the younger man, who, as always, was immaculately dressed. What flair he had! That, however, was definitely not the way to go, unless it was the way Jeremy wanted it to go, and he had certainly never indicated any such thing. Ah, well, at least she had Karl.

She found a vase for the dozen white roses. A Bach CD - by now she could identify some of the better-known composers – could be heard from the stylish Bang & Olufsen and seemed perfect for the informal formality of her hosts. It certainly made a nice change from the techno music that had blasted her eardrums the night before. She sipped her wine with not an inkling in the world that she was about to be skewered and kebabbed.

Jeremy on the other hand was not relaxed. In fact, he was dreading what was about to occur. This young woman had become an important figure in his life, and, he believed, he in hers. Their relationship was about to be blown apart, and it was his hand that held the detonator. The countdown had begun. He was not one to waste too much time on small talk, and he cut straight to the chase.

"Chloe, does the name Karl Janssens mean anything to you?"

He might just as well have struck her with the large vase. She gulped, and visibly blanched.

"The name doesn't sound familiar. Why are you asking?"

She wasn't the only one to feel that she'd been kicked in the guts. In that instant, with that lie, Jeremy realised beyond doubt that he had been betrayed. Utterly bloody shafted. There was no coming back. The hand had been dealt, he had opened the bidding and she had passed. And failed. A sacrifice was necessary.

"Well, he wants to have some business dealings with us, and as he's a member at King's Ransom, I thought you might have come across him."

Fuck, she thought, Karl the dickhead's been grafting behind my back! He'd sworn he wouldn't. Was this the deal he was rattling on about? Backtrack and quickly. Chloe re-bid.

"Oh, hang on, yes, I do remember him - we chatted a while back. He tried to come on to me, but I wasn't interested. A bit too smooth for my liking."

"That's odd. I believe he spent the night at your flat on Tuesday, and again last night. Has he become less smooth? Or have you just got to like smooth more?"

Chloe could not but be aware of the menace in his voice. That she was being watched upset her greatly. Worse, it frightened her. Every word pierced her like a lance. Oh, Karl, you've screwed me in more ways than one.

"What's he done, Jeremy?" She asked the question, but absolutely did not want the answer. It could only spell trouble, trouble writ large.

"Not a lot," said Jeremy, "Just been trying to hack into my - our - accounts, plus a bit of nasty blackmail on the side. Nothing serious. What's a couple of million quid between friends anyway?"

Chloe faced paled once again. This menacing, sarcastic man was not the Jeremy she knew. It took only milli-seconds for her to realise that their warm relationship had come to a grinding halt, and that she was in deep, deep shit. So deep she could smell it, almost taste it. She felt revoltingly ill.

It was time for Daniel to enter the conversation. "Let's not bugger around, Chloe – do you admit you set us up with your friend?"

Time to come clean.

"I admit that I was involved at first, but that was before I got to know you. When we got back from Santa Fe, I told him I wanted out, and he promised me months ago he wouldn't carry on with the scheme – he swore he wouldn't. I just wanted to make some easy money. You guys would have done the same. I never knew anything about blackmail. Ohmygod, what have I done? I'm so so sorry Jeremy, you have been so fantastic to me. I wanted to be worthy of you but I've fucked everything."

Chloe burst into a paroxysm of tears. It was one thing to have to own up to gentle, genteel Jeremy, no matter how angry he was; another matter altogether to be facing a man whose father killed people for pleasure. The shit had just got deeper and the only question was the depth. She took a breath and began at the beginning.

Her words sliced through Jeremy like a broadsword, as little Shelley's had done fifty-six years before. His solicitor, bloody pompous Sir Christopher Reed-Gibbs, had been absolutely *en pointe* - there's no fool like an old fool. Damn you, Chloe! For only the second time in his life, Jeremy had been hurt, badly hurt, and for the second time it has been a young female who had been the inflictor. It had taken him years to recover from Shelley, but he did not have years to get over this.

Daniel took control. "Here's what you are going to do now, Chloe. You are going to phone Janssens and tell him you are alone in this apartment. You are going to tell him that Jeremy has been checking his accounts and has forgotten to shut down his computer because he was running late for a meeting. The meeting is in Amsterdam, and he will not be back till tomorrow evening. You will tell him to come over immediately because this is the only chance he will ever get to hack into

Jeremy's accounts. If you slip up, Chloe, if you warn him in any way, you can kiss your pretty ass goodbye."

"What are you going to do to him?"

"The same as we will do to you if you don't totally cooperate."

He indicated a tall black man who had quietly entered the room. "Unfortunately, your friend has got himself in too deep. Michel here will take care of him and place him on my private jet, new passport included, that will ostensibly be flying to Manchester but will take off for Lagos instead, where one of my father's colleagues will be awaiting him. If he gives even the slightest trouble, he won't come back, but the sedative he will be given should ensure there won't be any."

"Are you going to kill him?"

Daniel shrugged. "Well, I'm certainly not. I'm not a killer, but my father is, and we really didn't want to involve him."

If she had been upset when she'd had that tiff with Karl, that was chaff. Chloe had no illusions but that blood would flow, and however much she liked Karl, she did not want it to be hers.

"What's going to happen to me, Daniel? Jeremy? Am I going to Nigeria as well? Please, Jeremy, Daniel, please don't hurt me."

Jeremy smiled. That smile frightened her more than anything.

Forty-five minutes later - the worst forty-five minutes of Chloe's life when not a single word more was said - the doorbell tolled.

As Karl entered the foyer, he was immediately impressed by the opulence and good taste of the decor. Wall-to-wall mirroring, plush pile carpets, an elevator that was almost soundless. If this was how the ugly fat bastard lived, he regretted he had under-priced the deal. Then he thought that whether one million or two, it would be small change if he could actually get into Jeremy's bank account. He was going for the jackpot, and Chloe had come up trumps when the opportunity was there for the taking. Why had he ever doubted her? After all, it was she who had initiated the project, and even if she had wavered, she was obviously still up for it. Bees' knees, Chloe!

The door to the penthouse was open. The room was empty. He looked around – he'd been in one or two smart homes before, but this pad was in a different league. He knew nothing about paintings, but instinctively felt that the big one over the hearth could probably get him out of debt on its own and keep him going for a good while after that. He wasn't wrong; it was an early Andy Warhol, probably worth eight figures.

Then Chloe walked in. She looked wretched. Eyes, red; hair all over the place going every which way. He had never seen her like this. She said nothing. She wouldn't look at him. This did not feel good, in fact it looked a real mess. His immediate reaction was to get the hell out of there. He tensed. She flinched. Was she scared he would start smashing things up?

No way – don't get side-tracked. He relaxed a little. This wasn't about Chloe, and if she was having second thoughts, well tough titty. Do what you've come to do.

"It's no good Karl, they know all about it - we're fucked."

"Have you ratted on me, you stupid bitch? I've got a good mind to smash your face in."

As he moved towards her, arm raised, his attention was diverted - a short stout man entered the large lounge.

"Good evening, Mr Janssens, welcome. Have you come to collect your wage packet?"

His tension eased. Was this tubby little load of lard actually going to take him on? He could sort Jeremy out in less time than he needed to think how he would do it. How should he teach the fat boy a lesson he would never forget? Punch his lights out? Deck him? Just don't hit him too hard, he'd fold like a collapsing deckchair. One or two blows to the gut should be enough to make Jeremy see reason. Don't fuck with Karl Janssens, you stupid prick!

A far bigger shock did not take long to arrive. Two tall black men emerged. One, he recognised from his research - Daniel Odenfemji. The second man moved towards the elevator door. The tension returned, this time with interest. Time to get out of there. He looked towards the door. The guy standing there guarding his escape route was a brute. Karl was himself tall and well built, but he did not fancy his chances against this ogre. He was beginning to shit himself. Better to try and brazen his way out.

"I wasn't expecting to see you, Mr Lawson, but I'm pleased to meet you after all this time."

"Care for a drink, Mr Janssens? You look like you could do with one. What brings you here this evening?"

"Chloe asked me to come over because she fancied a shag in your very big bed that she keeps talking about. She says you don't put it to enough use."

Jeremy said nothing.

"But seeing you're in, perhaps I should be going."

"No rush dear boy, have a glass of best red with me – at £450 a bottle it should be at its prime. Should be a novel experience for you – I believe Jägermeister's your tipple of choice."

"What I'd like is to leave right now. I shouldn't be here."

"Quite right, you shouldn't. You will walk out of here in due course on your own two feet since we have no wish to cause you bodily harm. We are gentlemen after all. But first, a toast, to a clever ruse that almost succeeded. You did your research on my property dealings with great thoroughness, and your computer skills are formidable. Without wishing to sound condescending, are you sure you don't want a job in my security division?"

Karl could hardly refuse the glass of ruby-red wine. He took a very small sip – he knew immediately it was drugged. "Sorry, not my style." It would be last sentence he would utter for the next few hours. As he reeled, Jeremy took his wine-glass - no sense in ruining an expensive silk carpet. Michel stepped forward to take his weight and steer him into the elevator. It would be the last time Chloe would set eyes on him.

Daniel stood in front of her. "Your turn, Chloe. What shall we do with you?"

Chloe said nothing. All she could think of was how she had ruined her life: Karl gone forever. Jeremy's patronage at an end. Daniel and Kristina's friendship lost. How could she possibly have thought to attempt to outsmart a man whose brain was a computer, whose words were a razor?

Jeremy had saved the deepest cut for last. "You need to know something, Chloe. I'm dying. I have maybe a year to live if I'm lucky. You are the only woman that I have ever loved, and if you were unaware of that, then more fool you. You brought emotions into my life that I never knew I was capable of experiencing. Not lust. Pure simple love. Because of my feelings for you, I instructed my solicitor to put into my will that on my death he should deliver to you the sum of twenty million pounds."

Chloe instinctively knew a massive car crash was about to happen, and she would be the victim.

Jeremy paused briefly. "That would have been the good news."

Chloe went ash white. What was the bad news? Were they going to dispatch her as well? She'd behaved terribly but she didn't deserve to die for it. Or were they going to smash her up like they did to those Spaniards? If they messed up her face, she'd want to die anyway ...

Jeremy continued. "Unless I snuff it unexpectedly tonight, my lawyer will be informed in the morning that such a bequest is not to happen. In fact, why wait until the morning? I'm going to text him after you leave."

Chloe let out a deep breath of relief - she wasn't going to be killed. But they could still hurt her.

"Think about that, Chloe, twenty million pounds that was almost yours. Moreover, I was also about to offer you the opportunity of becoming the recipient of my not insubstantial pension. Even that would have given you more every month than you have ever earned. Think how your life and that of your sister and mother would have changed."

Her head began to swim. Could this be true? She had never known Jeremy to tell porkies. Then the reality hit her. Twenty million quid down the tubes ... a fat pension. A bitter taste filled her mouth. She felt sicker than she had ever felt in her life. She wanted to throw up but in her mind she thought it would ruin the carpet and Jeremy would be upset. She somehow managed to control herself, keep what was inside her inside.

Jeremy's voice was soft now, barely audible. "Were I a more vindictive person, I might have arranged to have your pretty face re-decorated, but that is not my way. Suffice it to say that you will never accompany me anywhere ever again. You will not ever accompany Karl anywhere either. And you will keep your mouth tightly shut if you don't want to end up in prison."

Jeremy wouldn't even look at her – she felt utterly diminished. She was beneath contempt. That hurt most of all. Everything gone. Maybe even her life if, after all, they chose not to spare it. At that moment she didn't much care. She had royally messed up, and Karl had finished the job. Karl was finished, and she was going to be as well.

Daniel took up the one-way conversation. "This is how it goes from here: you will walk to the elevator. You will leave the building. Where you go, we do not care. You will tell no one of the events of tonight unless you want a visit from Michel. You will spend the rest of your life ruing what you have lost. We will not see or hear from you ever again. Leave now, and be thankful it's not in a box. Goodbye, Chloe."

Jeremy did not, could not watch her leave but heard the faint sound of the elevator door closing. Something within him was closing too or had already closed.

Chapter 35

Aftermath

The next few weeks were pure hell for both Jeremy and Chloe.

The very last thing Chloe wanted to do was to carry on her regular visits to the King's Ransom, but she was intelligent enough to realise that if she did not, questions would be asked, highly embarrassing questions. She had to continue going there and be as surprised as anyone else that Karl wasn't making his usual appearance. She said nothing to her mother. She said nothing to her sister. Who knew what might unintentionally slip from their mouths - another visit from the Nigerians didn't bear thinking about, and she knew they meant it. And if Luke even became slightly suspicious... so she just carried on looking more and more sad, which wasn't at all difficult given how she felt.

THE MAIL ON SUNDAY

POLICE INQUIRIES FAIL TO TRACE MISSING FOOTBALLER

Despite an on-going and intensive search for one-time Charlton Athletic footballer Karl Janssens, the head of the search team, DI Sam Wollastin, has been forced to admit that they have made little progress. Janssens was reported missing three weeks ago by his erstwhile team-mate Luke Simmons, but so far not a single trace has been found. Mr Simmons has told police that Janssens was deeply in debt through gambling and betting, and it is feared that Mr Janssens has either been the victim of a gangland assassination by racketeers or has taken his own life.

Another possibility is that he has pulled a Lord Lucan and simply disappeared, leaving everything he possessed behind including his passport.

The police have also questioned his girlfriend, Ms Josie Buttler, but she too has been unable to shed any light on the mysterious disappearance of a once promising footballer. She was said to be shocked and saddened by his disappearance.

DI Wollastin has promised to leave no stone unturned and was sure that they would sooner rather than later bring the search to a successful conclusion.

When Chloe read this, she retched. She was retching a lot these days. Who the hell was Josie Buttler? Had Karl been two-timing her? Well, it was pretty damn obvious that he had been. Fuck you, Karl, I hope you rot in hell.

As for Jeremy, it was difficult to determine which pain was causing him more grief, that from his swollen and rotten prostate or what was left of it, or from the other organs to which the cancer had spread, or his heart which was broken from the betrayal. The morphine he was prescribed did somewhat alleviate his bodily pain, but, if anything, exacerbated the turmoil in his head. Regret wasn't an emotion regularly experienced by Jeremy, and he felt nothing about his act of commissioning the disappearance and probable murder of his nemesis, Karl. On the other hand, the bouts of anger towards Chloe were tempered by his conflicted feelings of sadness and regret in those final months of his life. Had he been too harsh with her? She was just a product of her times, trying to do the best she could with whatever assets were available to her.

How much easier would his last months have been without this torment. Did he have it in him to forgive her? Ask her to sit by his side as he eked away? Re-instruct his solicitor? He dismissed these fatuous thoughts. It was over for them, over for him.

Never before had he been bothered by loneliness, but he would have welcomed the sight of her face, what he had thought of as her innocent face. Words came floating into Jeremy's mind, words he had not thought of since studying Hamlet at school:

"The spirit that I have seen may be the devil: and the devil hath power to assume a pleasing shape."

He stared up at the unyielding ceiling at the hospice. Ceilings don't say much...

Obituary: The Times

Sir Jeremy Lawson

Sir Jeremy Lawson, property developer and philanthropist, received his knighthood just three weeks before his untimely death through prostate cancer. It is known that Her Majesty's Government allowed protocol to be broken to allow his investiture to take place at an earlier date than had been planned because of his illness.

His pathway to wealth as a property mogul was unblemished. He was renowned for extensive renovation and reconstruction of older buildings, often combining several smaller structures into larger emporia. In recent years his activities had extended abroad, and he had only recently completed the purchase of the magnificent Lansdowne-Burlington Building in downtown New York.

Sir Jeremy was a known gourmet and was to be seen at many of the world's best-known eating establishments. Amongst the attendees at his funeral were celebrated chefs from all over the world whose restaurants he had graced.

A long-term colleague of his, Mr Daniel Odenfemji, delivered an eloquent eulogy in church, speaking of Sir Jeremy's largesse in supporting many worthy causes.

Sir Jeremy was known to have befriended a young woman in recent years who it was said had become for him the daughter he never had. Ms Chloe Jenkins is the deputy manager of the Kings Ransom Club in Chelsea. Although the scandalmongers in the gutter press were quick to make snide comments about this relationship, it was well known that Sir Jeremy was a self-proclaimed "vol-celib" - a voluntary celibate.

Ms Jenkins was unable to attend his funeral but was interviewed the day after. She informed our reporter of his kindness and generosity and spoke of how the only reward he sought was to be found in the pleasure he took as he educated her about his twin passions, opera and gourmet dining. She hastened to add that by her own choice she had not been made a beneficiary of any part of his estate.

Although his will is still in probate, a reliable source has said that it is expected that, aside from a gift to his long-term doctor and solicitor - both old friends - and a bequest of the title deeds to The Lansdowne-Burlington Building in New York to Mr Odenfemji, all of Sir Jeremy's vast wealth had been bequeathed to a number of charities including a substantial donation to the Royal Opera House where he was a perennial patron. The newly refurbished stalls will be named in his memory.

His vast collection of art, including paintings by his late parents are to be donated to the Tate Gallery, and we are reliably informed that a retrospective exhibition of his parents' work has been mooted.

In the property world not always known for its spiritual qualities, Sir Jeremy Lawson's honesty and integrity stood out like a beacon. Not a single person could be found who had a bad word to say about him, and those are the words imprinted on his tombstone.

Even though Chloe was not given to reading The Times, one of the more erudite patrons at the Ransom was, had seen her name mentioned and brought it to her attention. Her first thought? What a load of bullshit - the man was a fucking murderer! Of course, she did not say so. She just said what a kind man he was.

Poor Chloe. There are few feelings worse than knowing that you were *that* close to becoming seriously rich and then having it snatched away from you. From a gregarious, ever-cheerful optimist, she had become lonely and somewhat embittered. Her temper had shortened in inverse proportion to the number of profanities that had come to litter her speech. Her *joie de vivre* had pretty much evaporated. Was this her cosmic karma writ large?

Should one feel pity for her? After all, before this sorry saga blew up in her face, she had made the decision that she had no wish to fleece her benefactor - it was only Karl's duplicity that had shafted her. Tough call. The jury is out and will not be returning anytime soon.

Chapter 36

Postscript

"Good Afternoon, King's Ransom Club, how may I assist you?"

"Good Afternoon. May I please speak with Miss Chloe Jenkins?"

"Who shall I say is calling?"

I'd rather not say, but it is very important."

"Please hold the line, I will try to locate her."

"Thank you."

"Hullo, this is Chloe, who'm I speaking to?"

"Good afternoon, Ms Jenkins, this is Sir Christopher Reed-Gibbs, senior partner at the legal firm Reed-Gibbs Braceworthy."

Chloe went white. A lawyer. What could he be wanting of her? Something to do with Karl's disappearance? She was about to put a quick end to the call when the lawyer spoke once more.

"I have some information that may be of interest to you. In fact, I know it will be, and it could be very advantageous."

"What is it?"

"I'd rather not discuss this over the phone. Would it be possible for you to drop in at my office sometime soon? I'm at St Pauls' Churchyard in the City."

"I'm very busy, I'm deputy manager here at the Club. Can't you come here?"

"No, I have certain papers in my office which are of significant interest to you, that cannot be viewed elsewhere. May I suggest this Friday at midday?"

"OK, I'll be there, but I shall be very annoyed if this is a waste of my time."

"On the contrary I think you'll find the visit very much to your benefit."

He terminated the call and Chloe took a deep breath. The pounding in her head was subsiding. About time she had a bit of good news. Chloe's heart began to beat faster and faster. It was practically galloping.

Chloe walked out of the underground station at St Paul's, and as she rounded the corner, like many before her, she was struck by the grandeur of the huge and imposing cathedral. The thought struck her that this was the first time she had ever been into the City. She'd heard that the men who worked there wore bowler hats, but the only hats she saw were those of the omni-present builders.

After a brief wait in a well-padded reception room – not to her taste but oozing old money - she was shown into the solicitor's office. Same again – dull but classy, especially the certificates. The highly-polished wooden desk must have been at least a hundred years old; she hoped the solicitor would be a bit younger but would not have bet on it – he had sounded a pompous prat on the phone. *This is Sir Christopher Reed-Gibbs.* She knew the type from the Ransom, older men looking for a bit of skirt, or preferably someone without a bit of skirt. Their fists were usually as tight as a nun's twat.

She was feeling extremely apprehensive and nervous as she stood there, and this worsened when a stern-looking very tall man walked in and invited her to sit. He was even more repulsive than she had expected. Were he any thinner and more bony, he might have been mistaken for a corpse; as dried up as a raisin. The blue veins on his bald head were matched by those on his neck, resembling tattoos gone rogue. Protruding out of his cigar-reeking unfilled suit, his hands were overridden by liver spots forming a bizarre Rorschach psycho test. Everything about him made her cringe. She had to stop herself from gagging. This was not going to be good.

"Miss Jenkins - "

"Please call me Chloe."

"Very well, er, Chloe, what I am about to say to say is strictly *entrez nous.* "

"What?"

"I'm sorry, strictly between us. Not even my secretary will be privy to the discussion we are about to have."

"You're scaring me."

"Once again, I apologise. You have no need to be fearful. Please relax, because what I'm about to say may change the course of your life in the most beneficial way."

"Well, can we get down to it because I have to get to work."

"After this discussion, you may never have to work again."

Once again, Chloe felt her heart pounding. What the fuck was this all about? She was soon to find out.

"Chloe, I am the solicitor who represented your late friend, Jeremy - Sir Jeremy Lawson."

Her immediate thought was to get the hell out of there as quickly as possible, but then he spoke.

"I am not sure if you are aware that it was Sir Jeremy's intention to endow you with a large sum of money."

"Well, he didn't, did he?"

"He may have, and may not have, and that is what we are about to discuss, but once again I have to remind you that what I am about to say must never be repeated elsewhere. I will need you to sign a short promise to that effect before we proceed."

"And if I don't?"

"Then you will leave and never know about the offer I am hoping to discuss. If you do sign it, however, I must warn you that should you break your word, you will end up in court. Oh, and by the way, there's also the matter of a certain gentleman's disappearance, about which I will say nothing more."

Shit, this *was* about Karl.

"Now you're really terrifying me. I think I'd like to leave." She started to rise.

"That would be extremely short-sighted of you. It would result in you losing out on a considerable sum of money."

Chloe sank back in the chair. He placed a page of headed paper in front of her.

She read it. It appeared harmless. She signed it.

The solicitor smiled. "Now we can both relax. Here is what I have to say: about three years ago, Jeremy Lawson instructed me to include an addendum to his will saying that you were to receive the sum of twenty million pounds on his death, this despite me warning him not to do so. Last year, he signed a second will that rendered the first will null and void, and that second will excluded you as a beneficiary. He never mentioned the reason why, and I did not ask. Suffice it to say he was extremely upset."

He continued, "Now we get to the nub of the matter and the purpose of my call. You see, Chloe, I have both wills in my possession." He held up two documents. "They are exactly alike, except for the addendum in the first will that is absent from the second. In a week's time, Sir Jeremy's last will and testament is to be filed from this office. The question is, which one of the two wills, the first or the second, shall I file? And that, dear Chloe depends entirely on what you decide."

"*What I decide?* What's it got to do with me? I'm not the frigging lawyer."

"You are about to learn why I have had be so careful to swear you to silence."

"Jesus, can we fucking get on with this please?"

"That was not quite the swearing I had in mind, and I'm not sure Jesus has much to do with this, but you may wish to say a prayer after I've finished. So here is a proposition I wish to put to you. There is an amount of twenty million pounds that could conceivably be on offer were the second will to disappear."

"I don't understand."

"I'll make it a simple as possible. If you are prepared to come to an accommodation with me that the twenty million pounds be split between us, then the second will shall cease to exist. I will burn it. You will then be richer by ten million pounds, as will I, and no one will ever know. Unless you are dumb enough to start shooting off your mouth, which I do not think will prove to be the case."

"And if I don't agree?"

"Then this conversation never took place; you will leave here with nothing, and the second will shall be lodged."

"Won't any one query it?"

"There are no relatives, no jealous brothers and sisters or disappointed lovers. Only one friend, and Daniel will receive exactly what he was expecting to receive, the Lansdowne-Burlington building. Jeremy's doctor will get his three million, as will I. Yes, Chloe, he valued you far more than either of us. Several charities will receive unexpected and undreamed-of windfalls. Daniel is the only person who could ask questions, but if he does, it could delay his own bequest by several years. That is the nature of probate. Daniel's a practical man. No, no-one will query it."

"How're you going to deal with splitting the money?"

"Don't you worry your pretty little head, my dear. You aren't the first and won't be the last."

"Then fifteen million to me. It's my money."

"You're greedier than I thought, Chloe, and that's saying something. It is not yours until I make it become so – I have that power over you. Furthermore, I'm the one putting my career at risk. I want that money because there's a lovely flat in Mayfair that's coming up for auction quite soon, so ten million each, and you have five minutes to think about it. Would you like some tea?"

Chloe did not want tea, thank you, but she did think about it. She did not think for long, unless two minutes is long. Ten million quid that was hers for the taking if she could only think straight. What would Jeremy have advised her to do? Take the money! The thought of giving the other ten million away to this pompous shithead of a lawyer made her want to throw up on his desk. What right did this slimy snake have to ask, no, to demand anything of her, let alone *half* of what was due to her. *Half?* Greedy fucking bastard!

Then reason set in. She quickly came to the realisation that no matter how resentful she got about the lawyer, she would *never* see the half that he was proposing to keep; and if she didn't play ball with this tall pile of turd - she did not know that shit could be piled up so high - she wouldn't see the other half either.

On the other hand, the half that she would see if she co-operated would go a very long way indeed. With ten million quid, she could buy a share in the King's Ransom. The club really was appropriately named. Or she could develop her own club, she knew how to do it. Not in the King's Road but there were plenty of other less expensive sites. She could buy a two-bedroom flat in Battersea with the change. Or, if she preferred to stay at the Ransom, she could get a three-bedroomed flat in Chelsea and still have shedloads of money to live more than comfortably for a very long time. And travel – so many places she'd love to visit.

Decisions ... not about whether to take the money or not, of course she'd take it, rather how she could go about spending it. Shame Karl wouldn't be around to enjoy her legacy, but she never liked him that much anyway, and she was getting on really well with this film director she'd met at The Ransom ...

The beginning.

Acknowledgements

I thank my editors, Felix Hodcroft and Shyama Pereira, for their wisdom and for pushing me forward.

I thank my wife Adrianne Morris for her forbearance, patience and encouragement.

I thank Norman Jonas for proof-reading and Brenda Van Niekerk for type-setting the text.

I thank Susan Light for designing the cover

Thanks to Matt, Gavin and Bev for their support and interest, and to my friends who had the kindness to read and comment critically on the story, especially Prof Cyril Meyerowitz.

I thank all of you who have bought this book, read it and re-viewed it.

Thanks, Everyone!!!

About the Author

Ed Bonner was born and educated in Johannesburg, South Africa, where he graduated as a specialist prosthodontist in dentistry. He has lived in London for many years. He is an expert witness in medico-legal cases and has given evidence in court and at tribunals on many occasions. This combined with his extensive experiences in South Africa form the backbone of his first published story, **Trouble Will Find You** (Amazon & Kindle), and in his factional autobiography, **Open Wide**, to be published soon. There are four others to follow.

Trouble Will Find You

The fall of a talented facial surgeon is at the heart of '**Trouble Will Find You**.'

Dr Nick Simpson from Ballarat Australia is awarded a scholarship to study at University College London. His prodigious skill with a scalpel leads him to become chief surgeon at a prestigious hospital in Leeds. He and his solicitor wife are much admired. He is at the top of his game. Inexplicably, Nick goes through a crisis of self-doubt. He becomes addicted to an unnecessary medication, begins to forge prescriptions, and his career is almost ended by his disdain of ethical conduct. His life begins to spiral downwards. He has to appear before a medical tribunal where he is brought down by a vindictive female colleague and gets suspended from practising in the UK. However, he is allowed to work abroad and decides to seek a position in South Africa.

Dr Simpson attempts to resurrect himself and his career at a remote hospital in rural South Africa where he meets interesting people and experiences life in Africa with all its warts and beauty – snakes, witchdoctors, vultures, river rafting and exploding arteries. He develops a relationship with a young widow and her family who give him hope. Will he find redemption?

Amazon / Kindle Reviews of Trouble Will Find You:

What's most brilliant about this novel are the things that come, unfiltered, from writer Ed Bonner's brain and pen. It's a pacily-written, exciting and moving saga about fall and redemption. The characters are fascinating and resonant. You will learn much about advanced medical practice - and malpractice; about the tragedy of post-apartheid South Africa. And you won't be bored; not for a moment.

I loved the surgical detail - obviously the author knows his stuff!

I look forward to more stories from this talented writer.

This is an engaging book made very interesting given the author's deep and personal medical and legal knowledge .Written in a fast but nuanced pace, I quickly became absorbed in the charismatic protagonist's life and found it difficult to put the book down.

Imbued with the author's own rich life experiences, one travels alongside, learning about medicine, the law, unknown territories and colourful people, rejoicing in their highs, shattered by their lows, expecting the worst, but hoping for the best. A well-rounded story, this is a book I would highly recommend.

Ed Bonner is a storyteller par excellence. His deep understanding of the medico-legal world and of South Africa provides a context and a setting for Nick, the protagonist, to experience the fragility of career and the beauty of deeper self-understanding and of relationships. This is a book worth reading.

An absorbing story of how determination and character overcome troubles of many types which confront a man of special talents but lacking in real world common sense. The author's descriptions of events, adventures, political and legal matters are so alive they provoke the reader to contemplate them as if they were the victims.

Printed in Great Britain
by Amazon

39674624R00138